STRANDED IN SPACE

Nathan and his team worked together in the vacuum of space, constructing the rear section of the huge spaceship that would take them to Mars. As he held on to his end of the massive metal plate, Sergei used a special wrench to tighten the bolts so Gen and Lanie could weld it in place with the space arc welder.

Suddenly the torch light went out. "Gen," Nathan radioed, "what happened?" But he got only static, then total silence. There was nothing scarier than the total quiet of deep space.

Gen motioned with his heavy suit arm that his radio was dead and moved toward a nearby metal strut. The others took his cue and touched their helmets to the strut, remembering what Dr. Thompson had said about sound waves traveling through the metal into their helmets for emergency communications.

"We've got only twenty minutes left of air!" Gen said. "Without radios we can't call for help."

"Yeah," Lanie said. "Don't waste oxygen talking. Let's get back to *Icarus*."

Nathan gave the thumbs-up signal and led the team to the space thruster sled. Lifelines checked, magnetic boots locked in place, Karl hit the green ignition button. Nothing happened. It was totally dead.

Stranded, Nathan thought. They were stranded in deep space.

D1605984

BLAST OFF WITH THE FIRST TWO ADVENTURES
OF THE YOUNG ASTRONAUTS

THE YOUNG ASTRONAUTS   (3000, $2.95)
Nathan thought it would be the coolest thing in the world
to travel to another planet. And after actually *making* it to
the semifinals in the United Nations' special program to
send young people into space, he couldn't believe his team
was screwing up the training program!

At the Houston Space Center, they were supposed to be
learning the skills they would need to colonize the Red
Planet. Instead, Nathan's group was labeled as the trouble-
making team.

The Survival Trek was coming up fast, and those who
failed would never leave the earth. There would be no ex-
cuses for those who lost. But those who won would become the youngest astronauts in the world!

THE YOUNG ASTRONAUTS #2:
BLASTOFF   (3173, $2.95)
Nathan and his crew proved themselves worthy: they have
made it into space. They should be able to sit back and enjoy the ride. Well, not exactly.

Their first stop is the space orbital platform that rotates
around Earth. Zero gravity takes some getting used to —
and so does living in close quarters with teammates like
flirty Noemi, wild-and-crazy Gen, sarcastic Lanie, ladies'
man Sergei, sensible Alice, and arrogant Karl. But they
have real work to do — building the three colony spaceships
that will take them all the way to Mars.

Then a cable snaps during a routine space walk and they
come close to losing a few crew mates to the relentless drift
of space. That's just the first of a series of mysterious mal-
functions that threaten their mission — not to mention their
lives. But whether it's sabotage or something even more
dangerous, they have only themselves to depend on. . . .

*Available wherever paperbacks are sold, or order direct from the
Publisher. Send cover price plus 50¢ per copy for mailing and
handling to Zebra Books, Dept. 3178, 475 Park Avenue South,
New York, N.Y. 10016. Residents of New York, New Jersey and
Pennsylvania must include sales tax. DO NOT SEND CASH.*

JACK ANDERSON PRESENTS...

THE YOUNG ASTRONAUTS

#3 SPACE BLAZERS
RICK NORTH

ZEBRA BOOKS
KENSINGTON PUBLISHING CORP.

RL 5.6 IL age 10 and up

ZEBRA BOOKS

are published by

Kensington Publishing Corp.
475 Park Avenue South
New York, NY 10016

Copyright © 1990 by Jack Anderson

All rights reserved. No part of this book may be repro-
duced in any form or by any means without the prior written consent of the Publisher, excepting brief quotes used ir
reviews.

First printing: November, 1990

Printed in the United States of America

Chapter One

The image on the screen was both familiar and unreal. There, suspended in the blackness of space, hung a single brilliant sphere. It was shimmering blue with white clouds swirled over the top like marshmallow frosting. There were patches of brown and bits of green studded in the endless oceans.

Under the screen was a yellow bumper sticker that read "Happiness is Earth in your rearview mirror."

Nathan Long wasn't sure he agreed. Happy as he was to be in space, there was something a little lonely and sad about the planet on the view screen. Maybe because he couldn't see anything human from this distance. During the planetary night the lights of the cities were easy to see, and then everyone on the team tried to pick out home.

Nathan knew that there was no way he'd find his own town, but the nearest city was Chicago, and even that was hard to locate at night, when he couldn't make out the Great Lakes. It was easier when the surface was bright and the clouds were just whispers in the atmosphere.

He couldn't see Chicago now, or even where it should be. He was looking at the Pacific Ocean spread over the globe with Japan just coming into view. It was a good thing his teammate Genshiro Akamasu was listening to a CD with his eyes closed. Gen claimed not to be homesick, but he always got real quiet when he saw Japan floating below.

Nathan knew exactly how he felt, but Nathan at least didn't try to hide it. He didn't have to. He wasn't cool like Gen with his long hair, heavy metal CDs, and attitude.

It wasn't all homesickness though. There was the fact that Earth seemed so small and fragile from here. And so alone. From this screen on the shuttle *Hermes*, it was clear that the planet was mostly water. Three quarters was the accurate count, but it looked like so much more, as if the continents were just big islands surrounded by the sea.

"Look," Alice said. She was hanging on the hand grip next to Nathan and nudged his elbow, pointing to the corner of the screen. She wasn't pointing at her own home, New Zealand. Instead, she had picked out one of the struts of the orbital platform *Icarus*, which was their destination.

The research space station *Icarus* was the last part of their training before their actual blastoff to Mars. Along with the more than four hundred other young astronauts and their supervisors in the program, they would learn to get used to living and working in a total deep-space environment.

"Should we get everybody?" Nathan wondered aloud. Maybe they should pull on the official jump suits and strap into their seats. The T-shirts and shorts that were standard wear aboard the shuttle weren't regulation for docking with the orbiting station.

"They'll tell us," Alice said. She was right. "What I'm worried about is Karl. He's still sick."

Nathan shook his head. They'd all been spacesick the first day. The pilot and commander aboard the shuttle had reassured them that absolutely everyone got spacesick the first time in zero-G, even with all their training in self-hypnosis and biofeedback. "Your whole body loses its bearings and doesn't have a reference point. We evolved in gravity and our bodies like to know which way is down. But you'll get used to it."

Most of the team managed to get past it in the first few hours, all except Noemi and Karl. Noemi had simply quit eating anything and moaned in a corner. Karl had been miserable. Nathan couldn't help feeling very sorry for both of them as he learned to adapt to weightlessness.

It was the most wonderful feeling he could

7

imagine, once his stomach stayed in one place. No position was uncomfortable. Standing and lying down were exactly the same. He could drift with no effort or he could push off a wall and fly across the space.

As a matter of fact, he and Gen and Sergei had been playing Superman in the cargo bay as soon as they recovered, which had given them a little practical experience with the law that for every action there is an equal and opposite reaction. They had been pushing off the wall (or whatever surface it was, walls and floors and ceilings all being the same) and zooming across the space, hands held out in front of them just like Superman in the comic books. Only Nathan had misjudged and had let go before getting enough push. He had been stranded, floating, in the middle of the bay. He tried to kick as if he were swimming, but that just made him go in a circle, head over heels.

The cargo bay was the biggest open space aboard the *Hermes*, and even packed with building materials there was plenty of room. Too much room. He couldn't get a hand or foot on anything. The more he flapped his arms and legs, the more he spun around.

For a moment Nathan had panicked. It was like the time he had been coming down the Chesterman Street hill on his skateboard, full tilt, when he saw a car run the stop sign. He knew then, very clearly, that he was going to be hurt as he cut the turn too sharply. He'd been thrown from the board and gotten a sprained ankle and scalp wound that bled all over the place.

Someone called his mother at work, and she got into trouble with her boss for taking off early to get him to the hospital. Seven stitches later he decided that he could have cut the turn a hair wider and kept his weight closer to the ground and he would have been fine. The laws of physics were immutable. Unfortunately, he had figured this out too late. His fear had made him act suddenly, before he could think things through.

And he was doing it again, flailing around in the cargo bay without thinking. Like an animal that didn't know even basic mechanics.

"Hey, Nathan, hold on," Sergei called from across the bay. Then the Russian boy launched himself at Nathan and sped across the open space. When he got to Nathan he just gave him a push. Nathan found himself moving toward a packing cage and held out his feet. He used the packing cage to push off again, and this time he had enough directional energy to make it to the far wall, panting.

Then Gen had launched himself, screaming like Tarzan.

"All right, hold on," a voice came over the intercom. "Just sit tight and we'll be right there."

The three of them cracked up.

"Way to go, Gen," Nathan said.

"Let's get out of here before they come," Sergei suggested.

His idea didn't need seconding. In less than a minute they were through the hatch and back into the cramped passenger area of the shuttle.

That was when they discovered the screen and were transfixed by the view of Earth. Sergei was certain that he could lócate his home city of Leningrad on the land mass of Europe and Asia. They hadn't even noticed when Lanie and Alice and Noemi came in. Karl was in the head being sick.

"No countries," Lanie had said, awed. "You see how artificial our borders are from here."

"And real," Sergei said softly. He pointed to the rivers and mountains. "They're pretty from here, but those mountains are so high you can see their white peaks. And we can't see anything man-made. You have any idea how big these mountains are?"

"You're wrong," Alice said firmly. "You can see the Great Wall of China. See, over here. It's sort of like a river over the mountains."

The Great Wall held their interest for a while, but then everyone was more interested in looking for home. The Soviet Union was a white expanse overcast with clouds. They didn't need Sergei to tell them that the thaw hadn't touched the north, where his family lived. Nathan wished Karl would get in there so he could point out his home in Frankfurt, Germany. The globe was still

10

turned so they couldn't see the islands of Japan or the Western Hemisphere yet.

"You know, it doesn't look real at all," Lanie said. "I mean, it's just like on TV or special effects. Not real high-tech ones either."

Fifteen hours later the magic still hadn't worn off. Nathan hadn't thought about looking at the moon or the stars. Earth alone was enough to hold his attention forever, it seemed.

From this viewpoint Nathan felt that life was very sacred. There was just a small set of conditions that all combined to create the water and the first single-celled plants, then the algae and the sea animals that eventually crawled out of the water. All the life in the solar system was concentrated here, where it was neither too hot nor too cold, where there was air with the right amount of oxygen and nitrogen, where the planet had a molten core and a hard rock crust and seas. The only place where anything lived in the solar system. Maybe the only place where anything lived in the whole galaxy. That we know of, at least, Nathan thought.

Soon the four hundred selected young colonists would make a home on Mars. Someday people would stare into the night sky and know for sure that in all the bright lights they weren't alone.

A buzzing sound brought Nathan out of his daydream. The members of his team were already in their Mars-red jump suits, getting

11

strapped into their chairs. Even Karl, looking a little pale and unsteady, was working the buckles of his safety straps like a pro.

Nathan had to hustle to pull on the jump suit over his shorts and T-shirt and get strapped in before the red warning light went on. There was no sensation at all, and then a jolt that vibrated through his bones.

"*Hermes* arrived. We have achieved docking position and are adjusting the seals."

Nathan heard the words. He knew intellectually that the ship and the station were both fully pressurized. Three separate seals had to come to full pressure before they would open and the shuttle travelers could swim onto the orbital platform that would be their temporary home. He knew about air pressure and the vacuum around them, and he knew that there were two backup systems just in case. And he also knew that if each of the seals didn't respond to full air pressure, their docking would abort and they would have to try again.

He was scared anyway. After the launch, this was the most delicate part of the journey. Here the couplings had to join perfectly, and a fraction of a millimeter could mean death. They had come so very far, and so very little could kill them. Space had Nathan's full respect, not just as an adventure, but as an enemy.

A blue light flashed. "*Hermes*, you are go for entry. Repeat, you are go."

The young astronauts all cheered and clapped. And then the pressurized door opened and they could see the inside of the station. They unbuckled the safety rigs and gathered by the door.

"Well, who's going first?" the commander asked jovially.

"Me," at least four of the young passengers said at once, and began to crowd through the opening. Laughing, they fell back and formed a line. First Nathan, who, after all, had been elected team leader back in Houston when they were in the final selection phase. Then Sergei, who was Nathan's best friend. The two of them always seemed to do everything together. Then came Noemi and Lanie, squeezing through together. They were a strange pair, Noemi, who looked like a movie star with her thick dark curls and her perfect makeup, and Lanie, who was from a poor family and looked more like a street tough than an ace hacker. Karl followed, making sure not to hold on to the door frames. He might have been spacesick longer than the rest of them, but he was too proud to show it. Alice was next and Gen was last. Not because he necessarily wanted to be last, but because he wasn't going to let anything ruffle his attitude.

They were a great team, Nathan thought proudly. Not just because they were smart and able to handle trouble. That would have made them only good. They were great because they were family. Even when they were angry at each other, they still were united against anyone on the outside.

Nathan was an only child. Suddenly he realized that he had six sisters and brothers. This was very different from when he arrived by bus at the Johnson Space Center in Houston. All the members of his team had been in that group, and they had all been strangers. And they had been wound up tight, wondering who among them was going to make the final cut and go to Mars.

"Oh, no, what did we do wrong now?" moaned Sergei, and Nathan realized that someone else had come into the small docking chamber. It was Dr. Lawrence Thompson, and Nathan wasn't thrilled. Their supervisor was not exactly their biggest fan.

"Well," Dr. Thompson began sternly, "you made it here. Believe it or not, I'm happy to see you all. As you may know, this platform is not just our staging ground to Mars, but supports a number of other U.N. space science projects as well. Which means that you had better not mess up someone's experiments. Okay. Now, if you'll follow me, we'll get you settled in. This isn't luxury, you know. And keep a grip on the rails at all times. You still don't have your space legs, and I don't want anyone getting hurt." With that, the tall black supervisor turned and led them through a door into the station proper.

"What's his problem?" Noemi whispered. "We

14

can't get into trouble here. We don't have the Mercedes."

Nathan tried not to laugh and succeeded only in choking.

"You know what I think?" Gen asked jauntily. "I think he kind of likes us. I think he likes our spirit because maybe he's got a little of it himself."

"You're crazy," Karl responded. "He thinks we're irresponsible. Again. And if he's right, this time I'm not taking any of the blame."

"Hey, stop being such a wet blanket," Alice hissed. "We've made it. We're here. Shut up and enjoy it."

Chapter Two

The boys dormitory aboard the *Icarus* was no different from the one on the shuttle. There were fifteen sleeping hammocks tethered to the wall, three rows of five. And there were fifteen locker compartments for them to put their personal belongings. Somehow it seemed very bleak.

Nathan didn't have much. None of them did. There wasn't room. Genshiro had his electric guitar, which was too large to carry with him according to the instructions they had been given, but most people were a little loose about music. Nathan himself had nearly fifty CDs, which along with his skateboard and a couple of T-shirts were about the only personal items he brought. Not counting his toothbrush, of course. Karl had brought several books of sheet music by composers whose names Nathan recognized — Schumann, Chopin, Debussy, Liszt, Vivaldi.

Gen strapped his guitar inside his hammock and glanced over at Karl's collection. "Vivaldi?"

he asked, surprised. "I play some of that stuff. Bach. I know some Bach on the guitar."

Karl looked so surprised that Nathan thought he was going to get sick all over again. "But all you ever listen to is heavy metal. Besides, I never heard anyone playing Bach on an electric guitar."

"Well, maybe you haven't heard of everything in the world," Gen said with a grin to let Karl know that he wasn't getting ragged out. Karl was sensitive, and the team hadn't completely gotten over all the hard feelings from Houston when Karl had nearly turned Lanie in to Dr. Thompson.

"But we're not in the world anymore," Sergei pointed out. "We're in orbit. We're in space." Sergei held one of the hammocks as he positioned himself against the wall, then shot out through the tangle of fabric to complete a perfect somersault in the middle of the dorm.

"Hey, watch out," Gen cautioned.

But Karl took the cue. Holding two of the sleeping bag lines, he positioned himself and pushed out into a backflip, landing in his original position. Nathan applauded. Karl had the highest physical rating of the whole team, and it looked like he had gotten over his earlier bout of spacesickness.

Nathan was tempted to try a trick when Dr. Thompson reappeared. "The girls are waiting for you down in Lounge D, which is at the yellow end of the access tube. You'll be meeting your partner teams and we'll explain what's going on."

Gen had already changed into a faded Metallica T-shirt with the sleeves torn out, shorts, and Velcro-heeled socks. Not to be outdone, Nathan pulled on his favorite Powell shirt, the one with the snakes. Only Karl still wore the red jump suit that was their project uniform and work suit. He eyed the other boys with disdain.

They had to get to the yellow area. The corridor was painted bright red. They found a vertical access tube with handgrips down one side. It started at red at the floor, faded down to orange, then yellow. Nathan began to climb down the grips, but it was harder than he thought. There wasn't any gravity to help, and so he had to push from one to the next.

"Hey, Nathan, go faster," Sergei yelled from the top of the tube.

He didn't have to touch every grip. With a good enough push he could pass two or three before he needed to reach out again. It was much faster. As he descended he was passed by an adult in the U.N. space uniform, diving head-down.

Of course, there was no reason for him to be going feetfirst except habit, because he wouldn't fall. Without gravity a lot of old habits wasted time and energy.

Nathan looked into the yellow area, calculated

how far it was, and shoved hard off the hand-grip. When he found himself surrounded by yellow, he grabbed back on and steadied himself at the right level to float through the door.

Lounge D wasn't hard to find. A bright green sign in five languages labeled their meeting place. For the space station it was large. Small monitor screens were scattered over every surface, and there were Velcro-covered struts in front of them. There were also fourteen strangers in the room, along with the three girls from their own team. All seventeen teenagers were using the Velcro patches on their socks, wristbands, or waist pouches to anchor themselves to the walls and struts. Nathan floated over to the girls and used the Velcro heel of his sock to keep himself in place.

Dr. Thompson followed the team into the room and used his wristband to steady himself on the far wall. "Now that you're all here, we can begin with the first phase of our journey to Mars. As you know, we are on the orbital platform *Icarus*, where the three colony ships that will take us to Mars are being completed. It is easier to assemble them in space than to try to raise them into orbit from Earth's gravity well. For every kilo of payload, you burn up fuel and need immense thrust to escape velocity. Fully loaded colony ships would be too heavy to lift to speed, so we are assembling the pieces here.

19

"You will all be assisting in the process of building the ships. The engineers, of course, are in charge and will be taking care of the delicate systems. But as far as simply placing plating, welding, basic grunt-and-carry work, all colonists are involved. Not only are you here and available, but you also have to know these ships inside out. And you will have to be able to disassemble them once we reach Mars. It would be wasteful to abandon all the metal and electronics that are going into them to drift in Mars orbit. We'll need all the resources we can scrounge, especially in the first years.

"Also, it will give you all a chance to learn skills that will be important. Practical things like construction and mechanics, that most of you don't even think about.

"We're organizing groups of three teams each. Each of the teams was at a different site for the selection phase, so none of you know one another. We felt that was best to get the groups more integrated. Once we reach Mars, it won't matter who was in Houston or Geneva or Star City or Calcutta.

"You will find your schedule displayed on the screens around this room. I have another group to meet, so I'm going to give you some time to study the schedule and the layout of the station before Engineer Al-Wahab arrives to start your instructions." Pushing off to the open door, the supervisor left.

"We're going to be doing construction work?" Noemi moaned. "I didn't get involved in this to do construction work!"

"This is making me nervous," Lanie confessed. "I mean, how do we know that what we build is going to be good enough to get us to Mars?"

But Karl's eyes sparkled. "Getting to build a spaceship is almost as good as getting to ride one. And getting both . . ." He looked like he had just received a gift of a new car.

" . . . is a lot for the first day on *Icarus*," the tall, black girl next to Karl said quickly. "I mean, we're just getting used to this place and Thompson hits us with work details. What a drag."

"We are not here to rest, uh . . . what is your name?"

"Tara White, Gamma team by way of Houston and Harlem, New York City. You're with the Alpha team, right?"

"Yes, I'm on the Alpha team. My name is Karl Muller. These are my teammates."

"Hi. Guess we never bumped into each other at the Johnson Space Center. But it looks like we'll be working together up here. Thompson's got us all locked in pretty tight."

The duty schedule glowed on the monitors directly behind them. Tara was right. And, to make matters more complicated, they had to remember to reset their digital watches to station time, five hours later than Florida time.

"Hey, does anyone realize that it's dinner in Cape Canaveral right now," Sergei said. "I'm starving."

"Me too," a pretty girl with dark curls and big brown eyes said quietly in a soft French accent. Nathan turned to read her name tag: Lisette Dupres. "We haven't had anything to eat since blast off and that was hours ago."

"I think this calls for an exercise in team work," Nathan said.

"Like what?" Tara asked.

"A kitchen raid. I organized one in camp two years ago."

"Where is the dining hall?" Lisette asked, looking at him and smiling.

"There's one in Yellow Seven," Gen volunteered.

"Yeah, but the layout around here is crazy," Sergei said. "We could get lost."

Gen waved a hand. "No problem. I looked at the diagrams."

Nathan smiled. Gen's photographic memory was almost as amazing as his abilities to see through mathematical and physics puzzles. If Gen weren't so dedicated to always being just a bit weirder than anybody else, he could easily be a real goody-two-shoes dweeb.

Gen's pronouncement seemed to decide the

22

issue.

Decks were indicated by color, and sectors by number. At first Nathan thought it was a little cute, until he realized that the usual words like "up" and "down" meant nothing at all on the space station. The corridors were painted the appropriate color and had Velcro strips running down the center and handgrips on the sides, spaced widely. Gen ignored the Velcro and used the handgrips to propel himself securely to the turn in the corridor, then through the next sealed segment into a long narrow space with doors on every conceivable surface.

"This should be it," Gen announced.

"But this doesn't look like a kitchen," Noemi wailed.

"I'll bet all these boxes are cupboards. And if we open them up, we'll find food," Lanie said.

There was a labeling system, but Nathan couldn't read it. It wasn't in any of the official U.N. languages, or even pictograms. Just strings of letters and numbers. The first door Nathan opened was stacked with small plastic containers of beef stew. That looked promising. And the next had packages of thin crackers.

"Hey, look, here's a microwave," Lisette offered.

Nathan immediately gathered the stew containers and heated them for the group. Someone had found spoons and passed them around. Soon the air was filled with cracker crumbs floating around their faces.

"How are we going to clean this place up?" Alice asked.

Nathan hunted down the crumbs, which he squashed together in his hand and threw down the disposal. The containers and spoons were placed in the bin marked recycle. All in all, the place wasn't completely gross when they left it. Maybe no one would notice for a while.

"The food beats Houston," Gen said cheerfully.

"That's not saying much," Tara said. Everyone laughed.

They managed to get back to Lounge D moments before Al-Wahab arrived. The engineer was a slight, young-looking man with a thick mustache and glasses. His eyes flickered over the group as they got settled again.

"Hello," he said so softly that Nathan could hardly hear him. "Tomorrow morning we will begin training on various space construction techniques. I am assured that your previous training included E.V.A. preparation. Please note your schedules and places where we are meeting. It is a pleasure to work with you." And then he was gone.

"Well, that was strange," Lanie said.

"Did you hear? E.V.A.!" Sergei whooped so loudly, the room echoed.

E.V.A. Extra-Vehicular Activity. Even more than going into space in a ship or a platform, to actually wear a space suit and take a walk "outside" was something Nathan had dreamed about. And now the rabbity engineer acted as if it were the most obvious thing in the world. Only, to quote Sergei, they weren't in the world anymore.

Chapter Three

Lanie was staring out the observation bubble at the glowing Earth shown in full majesty. "Isn't it beautiful?" Noemi asked, sighing.

Lanie blinked. "I'm glad I'm gone," she said. "I don't want anything to remind me of Earth ever again. Maybe I'll even change my name, be a whole different person."

Noemi did not point out that Lanie had already changed her name to get into the program. There was something about the tough American girl that Noemi admired. Maybe it was her determination. Secretly, Noemi felt a little lost ever since they had arrived on the station. It was the third day and she hadn't had a chance to do anything that she was even vaguely good at. The others had practiced E.V.A. maneuvers with enthusiasm, but Noemi was sore from trying to move around in the bulky pressure suit. There was no place for her elegance, her style, her flair. And there was no real use just yet for her unquestioned brilliance in math.

When Noemi Velasquez looked around her, she saw thousands of pure mathematical forms. The relationships between them were clear and beautiful to her, the way a Norma Kamali dress was beautiful, or the diamond necklace she wore with her Ralph Lauren T-shirt. Her mother had given her that necklace as a good-bye gift. It would have been her wedding present.

But her talents were wasted when it came to constructing a spaceship. Even Gen's amazing memory worked just as well for basic plate placement and hull design as it did for the intricate lacework of algebra. Only Noemi, who was so used to always being the best where it mattered, whether that meant brains or money, felt useless and unneeded. She couldn't go so far as to say she was *unwanted*. Their team was too tight for that. But since she had consistently placed dead last in physical strength and agility, she knew she was holding them all back.

Now it was sort of a surprise to discover she wasn't the only unhappy member of the team. "I can't stand the way everyone just looks down there and drools, like Earth is the most beautiful thing in the universe, like it's the most wonderful life we ever had," Lanie was saying. "I didn't have such a great life. And I sort of wish that Karl would keep his mouth shut. Did you see the way Lisette looked at me yesterday? Like she felt sorry for me and didn't trust me all at the same time."

Lisette was the French-Canadian girl who led one of the other teams in their group. Lanie, Alice, and Noemi approved of the way she looked and envied the assured way she moved and led her team. And they hadn't missed the way Sergei and Nathan exchanged glances when she was around. It made them all a little jealous, and that was stupid.

"But I look so . . . so . . . I don't know," Lanie said, blinking her tear-bright eyes rapidly. "You're so beautiful and Alice is so capable and I'm just nothing. I look in the mirror and I see a kid from the projects. I don't know why. It wasn't like that before."

Noemi studied Lanie seriously. It was easier to think about Lanie's problem than her own. Worrying about a solution for someone else might at least take her mind off construction work.

Lanie looked just like Lanie. Her narrow, pale face and dark eyes were the same as they had always been, and her posture, which used to be the worst of all of them, wasn't too bad anymore — thanks to the lack of gravity giving them all an off-centered way of moving.

Noemi studied and thought. "It's your hair," she said finally. "It's almost grown out, and there isn't any stuff here to bleach it with."

That was the plain truth. Lanie's natural dirty-blond hair, which had always been bleached almost platinum blond, had a good two inches of white ends.

"I don't know why you bleached it anyway," Noemi chattered on. "Your natural color is pretty. And you're not going to get the chance to do it on Mars. You might want to think about just cutting off your ends. That would change you more than the name."

Lanie stared at Noemi for a long time. "You might just be right," she finally said. "It would make me different. But you don't know how to cut hair." This was a statement, not a question. Noemi hadn't even known how to do laundry when she arrived in Houston, and Alice and Lanie had constantly picked up her clothes from where she dropped them on the floor. If Noemi hadn't been so nice, she would have been impossible.

"No," Noemi agreed. "I can't cut hair. But Alice can. And we could do it with the minivacuum in the bathroom so it won't get into the ventilation system."

Lanie blinked. That was the most practical thought she had ever heard Noemi voice. "Sure," she agreed. After all, why not? Why should she dye her hair anyway, especially when Noemi was right. There wasn't going to be any Miss Clairol around for a very long time.

The girls found Alice in front of a study

screen. Noemi ripped her Velcro heel from the grip and pulled her wrist. "You're cutting Lanie's hair. Now."

"But I've got to catch up on the agronomy section," Alice protested feebly. Lanie snorted. Alice, who had grown up on a sheep farm, knew more agronomy than half the experts who were pretending to teach her. And Alice had the kind of sense where she knew exactly what would work. It was Alice who had known why they couldn't bring cows to Mars.

"They're too big," Alice had said. "And they eat too much. We could raise millions of chickens for what it takes to keep one cow."

Noemi got the little scissors out of her manicure set and the three girls huddled into the rest room. It was worse than tight, even without gravity. Every millimeter of space on the station counted. The rest-room facilities were bulky, convoluted vacuum devices.

The shower was the strangest of all. The zero-G toilet acted like a normal one, even if it worked on a completely different principle. But the shower, if you could call it that, was a large cylinder of plastic that closed around your neck on top and had a vacuum attachment on the bottom. The water didn't spray much at all, just sort of floated around like everything else in zero-G. Anyway, they were permitted only very little water, just enough to rinse off after using liquid soap. After air, water was the most precious thing aboard the *Icarus,* and water rationing was strict. The shutoff valve on the shower permitted each person no more than ten liters, or about three gallons, which was hardly anything.

In order to cut Lanie's hair, Alice climbed in the bottom of the shower vacuum. Lanie turned around so that her head stuck inside the enclosure and Noemi held her legs. She secured the enclosure loosely around her shoulders. Air could still get in but nothing as large as hair would get out before they got the system on.

Alice went to work. Lanie wished she could see what was happening. She wondered if Alice knew what she was doing. After all, Alice wore her own hair in long braids, usually pinned in a crown on her head in the weightless environment. She was not exactly Miss Fashion Queen.

Alice turned on the vacuum unit very briefly, cut again quickly, and vacuumed yet again. "I think that should do it," she said finally. "It's a little short, but it'll grow out."

Lanie and Alice pulled the shower enclosure off and stowed it in the collapsed position.

Noemi stared critically at Lanie for nearly a minute. "It's wonderful," she said finally. "Perfect. I'll bet no one will recognize you." And then she giggled.

Lanie couldn't wait to see what she looked

like. But there was only a tiny shaving mirror in the lavatory, so they went back to the dorm, where they had stretched a length of silver Mylar over the back of the door to make a full-length mirror.

Lanie stared at her reflection. The girl staring back had natural blond hair cut in a wavy page-boy. She looked competent and no-nonsense, just the way Lanie wanted to think of herself and never quite did.

"You'd look nice in earrings," Noemi pointed out. "You can borrow my sapphires if you want."

Lanie smiled and shook her head. She had just the right earrings for the girl in the mirror. She went to her locker and took out the only jewelry she had brought, a pair of small gold hoops.

Then she admired her reflection once more. No, the juvenile delinquent, the cheat, the person who hid her past, was gone. Now there was only one crack computer jockey any team would envy.

As it happened, they didn't see the boys until the next morning, or what passed for morning on the *Icarus*. They were supposed to meet down at the garden section. The hydroponic gardens aboard the *Icarus* served to produce both food and oxygen, just as the gardens aboard the *Nina*, the *Pinta*, and the *Santa Maria* would when they launched toward Mars. Without the garden there would be no trip and no colony.

They stood in the corridor in front of the garden area. No one went into the garden proper without a hydroponic engineer present.

"Are we all here yet?" Nathan asked sleepily, and yawned.

"Lanie's missing," Karl said. "Just like her not to show up on time and get us into more trouble."

"Get real, Karl," Lanie said. She was sick of his cracks.

His eyes flew open. "Lanie?" he asked, startled. "I didn't know it was you! You look so different. I mean, you look normal. I mean, respectable."

"If you get your foot any farther down your throat, you're going to gag," Alice informed him. "Why don't we press the buzzer and see if they're ready for us?"

That seemed as good an idea as any, so they let Alice take the lead. She came from a farm, so at least she would know the right kinds of questions to ask. All the rest of them were city kids, or from the suburbs, so the gardens were something of a mystery.

It was hot and humid among the plants. Nutrients were supplied in the fluid as the roots of

33

the plants drifted in space. It was eerie, Lanie thought. It reminded her of a horror movie. She didn't like the fact that she couldn't see far enough ahead through the lush plants to know what was up there, or even who was with her. And once the lecture started, she was really lost.

Now, a computer was a different matter. Put Lanie in front of a computer and there wasn't anyone in the program, no one at all who could beat her. There was nothing at all she couldn't do with a computer.

She was so wrapped up in her own thoughts that she didn't notice how miserable Gen looked until Noemi nudged her.

"Ask him what's wrong," Noemi said.

"You ask," Lanie countered.

Noemi shook her head. "He'll tell you. With me he just says everything is cool, or we talk about Boolean algebra."

Lanie didn't know what Boolean algebra was, and she wasn't about to find out. Instead, she sighed and wedged past Noemi to get to Gen. She tapped him on the shoulder lightly.

"Okay, what's the deal?" she whispered, aware that there was a lecture going on somewhere in the vicinity.

"Nothing," Gen replied.

"Suit yourself. But we can't do anything about nothing," Lanie pointed out. But Gen wasn't talking. He had turned to watch the agricultural engineer point to the broccoli. Lane turned off again, but then she remembered that she was the new Lanie, and the new Lanie was able to deal with anything. Somehow she'd find out what was bothering Gen.

After they left the gardens they had a recreation period in Yellow D. Lanie left the others and took over the terminal. Everyone agreed that was her unspoken right. She called up the games. Unlike Gen or the lecture on hydroponics, at least they made sense.

Chapter Four

"Like *Icarus*, the ships will be double-hulled and assembled with self-contained sections. This is in case any sort of leak develops. Of course, we want to guard against that possibility. A leak is the most dangerous thing that can happen in space. And since you will be passing through an asteroid belt on your way to Mars, we can't afford to take any chances," the engineer, Al-Wahad, was saying.

Nathan was barely listening. This was something he knew about. In fact, he and Sergei had talked about the dangers of the asteroid belt once or twice in the late Houston night when they couldn't sleep. If anything, Al-Wahad was understating the problem. Probably so they wouldn't get too scared, Nathan figured.

He remembered an experiment in one of

their space science classes. It had been a simple example of depressurization. When they created a vacuum in a can, the can had crumpled as if it had been through a compactor. Nature hates a vacuum, and any air rushes to fill the void. Even if the void is as big as all space.

But the main problem isn't just air. Otherwise a person could just hold his or her breath until he or she entered a pressurized space. No, the problem is pressure. Human bodies are built to withstand the pressure of the air pressing in. Take that away and they expand until they burst.

Right now the lecture was one of those general introductions before they got down to the interesting stuff.

Nathan was bored. Besides, there was something more interesting than the lecture in the large group. Lisette Dupres. She was a team leader and looked just as bored as he was. He had first noticed her in the kitchen raid.

He tried not to stare at her too much. Next to her sat his old rival, Suki Long. Nathan didn't feel Suki should have been chosen to go to Mars. She was smart, but then, every one of them was smart. It took much more than smarts to be a colonist. What Suki had were connections. Someone had pulled strings to get her included — probably to get away from her,

Nathan figured. Dr. Thompson had explained the political realities of the program to them and Nathan understood that they were just stuck with her.

"What about our specializations?" Tara White said, standing. The lecture was over and the question and answer period had started.

The engineer stroked his mustache. "Some of your specializations are not currently needed. Navigation, for example. Or geology or ecology. However, your work in those areas won't suffer, I am sure. You are all scheduled to do feedback monitor work on Galileo, the orbital telescope. And for those of you in computer work, well, we're going to need you nearly full-time just to burn in our systems. And you can consider this building phase part of your work in hardware. Agronomists will be on duty in the gardens, of course. We need our gardens on *Icarus* as well as the gardens we are establishing on the colony vessels. Is that all clear?"

"What I mean is," Tara said, "will we be spending all our time doing manual labor? I wasn't the top student in my district just to become a glorified welder."

The poor engineer looked pained. He blinked rapidly. "Well, no one is scheduled for more than a three-hour shift E.V.A. two or three times a week. One can hardly call that full-time construction. If you have an aversion to physical work, well, you would be better off in a university on Earth. There is going to be plenty of hard work on Mars. Anyway, E.V.A. is hardly a chore. It's something you should look forward to. However, if you feel different, perhaps we can arrange for you to return to Earth."

Tara sat down without another word.

"I'm glad I didn't say that," Noemi whispered to Lanie. "But I think she's right."

Engineer Al-Wahad continued. "The diagrams of the sections are in the daily file. Until you begin work shifts, it would be beneficial if you kept up with progress. We are very proud of the work we are doing here on *Icarus* in constructing the deep-space vessels," the engineer concluded.

Nathan sighed. In his opinion going to Mars wasn't deep space, even if it was past the lunar orbit. Deep space was something he would never see. No human was going to leave the solar system for another star in *his* lifetime, let alone the galaxy. No one ever could leave the galaxy—it was far too large—and hope to arrive in another one. Even at the speed of light they were thousands of years away.

"Hey, don't look so glum. It's lunch and the food here beats Houston by a few million degrees," Alice said.

Nathan looked up. Alice and Noemi were

standing next to him with a third girl who was vaguely familiar.

"Come on, Nathan, don't you recognize me?" the girl asked. "It's *me*."

He knew that voice. *"Lanie!"* he said finally. "Sure I recognize you!"

She gave him a mock punch on the shoulder.

"Well, at least she doesn't look like a delinquent anymore," Karl said.

The girls laughed. Then they all went to the Yellow 7 kitchen for lunch.

They had been formally introduced to the delicacies of eating in zero-G. Breakfast was fast and easy, but now there was serious food to consider. Each meal had been laid out in a tray that was heated and then unsealed. In a lot of ways it was like a TV dinner back home, only things tended to float away. And beverages were served in squeeze bulbs that looked like the things his mother used to baste turkey.

"After a while you get used to it," Dr. Thompson said. "Just like you get used to being weightless. As a matter of fact, sometimes when astronauts return to Earth they're so used to zero-G that they just leave glasses and things in the air. Of course, that means a lot of broken glasses."

"Use plastic," Gen muttered to those close enough to hear him. Noemi tried hard not to laugh but couldn't hold it, and the water she had been trying to swallow floated in a great glob into the room.

"Gross!" Lanie said in disgust.

Dr. Thompson took that as his cue to show them where the paper towels were kept. "It happens to everyone," he said reasonably. "Don't forget, you're all scheduled for two hours in the gym this afternoon."

"What's gotten into him?" Sergei whispered. "I thought he hated us."

Nathan shrugged. Dr. Thompson had been on their tails the whole time they were in Houston. Now, though, the real pressure started. Everything was life or death. Nathan couldn't help feeling overwhelmed.

The gym was at Red 17. It came equipped with three Exercycles and a strange array of rubber bands attached to the walls. Karl and Sergei started out in a cycling race, trying to rack up the most points fastest at top resistance. Alice took the third cycle, and the rest started to use the bands, stretching and pulling to work the muscles.

Noemi hated this. Especially when she chipped her bright silver nail polish on the band. Noemi was proud of her perfect nails and took care of them the way she took care of her hair, brushing it one hundred strokes every night.

41

The others were occupied and they wouldn't notice if she was gone for a minute or two. She edged away from the group and returned to the dorm.

In her cubicle she had a whole selection of nail polish. She pulled out the silver polish, unscrewed it, and began to daub a little on the chipped end. She didn't notice the thin stream of silver enamel that emerged from the bottle into the air.

When she finished, she held up her hand and turned too quickly. The bottle turned over.

No nail polish spilled out exactly. It floated in a glob, like the water. Only this was starting to get sticky. Noemi took a tissue and swatted at one of the smaller balls of enamel floating around. She got it, and a second one, but the long, thin wisp of silver had gotten away and was stuck to the underside of Alice's sleeping bag.

Noemi prayed that Alice wouldn't notice. She recapped the bottle quickly and threw it back in the cubby. By then it looked as if the whole compartment had been filled with silver rain.

Noemi didn't have the vaguest idea what to do. She tried to wipe up some of the spill with tissues, but they were spreading evenly and coating everything. One got tangled in her hair and she began to cry.

The universe was awful. What had she done, leaving home and her family and the house-keeper and all the things she was used to? This was worse than the fate her mother worried about so—that she was too smart for any man to marry and would have to become a nun.

Noemi would do anything rather than become a nun. Except marry one of the smiling idiots her father brought home from the ministry. At the time Mars seemed like the perfect answer to her future. No convent, no marriage to some junior functionary who wanted to curry favor with her father. Out of the whole thing.

Only, like most things Noemi did, she hadn't foreseen the reality of her situation. A reality that included a clump of silver nail polish hardening in her hair.

The young astronauts had gone through pressure-suit drill more than once, and now they were doing a practice run. They were going spacewalking for *real*, but not to do any work yet, just to get the feel of it.

Still, it was dangerous. One by one they clipped their line to the harness. Dr. Thompson was in the lead, followed by Noemi, who was the smallest and least physically agile. Then Gen followed as an anchor. Lanie, Karl, and Alice were next in line with Nathan after Alice. Sergei was last because he was the tallest and had the greatest mass. In gravity he weighed the most, but out here that didn't count. Mass, though, worked almost the same, in that a really massive object was harder to move than a smaller one. And a whole lot harder to stop.

Oxygen tanks were full and ready, the suits triple-checked. They were just going for a little tour of the platform and the solar sail.

The sail was neat. Karl had gone completely crazy over it and had explained it to everyone so many times that Nathan was ready to punch him. A thin sheet of Mylar held out stiffly reflected the solar radiation into the storage cells in the battery. Most of *Icarus'* power was supplied this way, free and always available.

Nathan stood in the air lock, surrounded by his team. Behind the dark visors he couldn't pick out who was who. The sunshields were down because they would be between Earth and the sun, and the unfiltered rays of light could blind a person. He recognized Dr. Thompson only because of his height. Their supervisor was half a head taller than anyone else.

Magnetic catches in the inflexible boots were engaged in addition to the safety line. The boots would adhere to the skin of the station but still allow easy movement. But even with all the safeguards there remained the fact that if someone did drift away, they would drift forever. Without gravity there was nothing to keep anyone in place.

The air lock cycled and they were in darkness. Then the outer doors of the station opened onto the startling brilliance of the sun. Even with his visor down, Nathan was dazzled by the light.

Space was not soft and dark like the night sky. Without air to blur the features of the galaxy, the stars shone crisp and clear and bright. Sunlight glittered over everything and reflected off the hull of the platform. Nathan was amazed. It wasn't like anything he had imagined. He had always expected space to be dark, like the night. He had forgotten that it wasn't so much night as always day. There was no sky because there was no atmosphere, but there was still light.

He heard Dr. Thompson's voice through the speakers in his helmet. "Always keep one foot on the station hull. Never jump for any reason. We're on a safety line and we're tied in to the main air lock. Every person aboard *Icarus* who does E.V.A. is required to take the same precautions. Now, if you will follow me, we're going to circle this strut of the station and go around to the dark side."

The speakers went dead and Dr. Thompson began to move out. He looked awkward, as if he were walking through a swimming pool, his movements slow and exaggerated.

Nathan discovered why when he tried to walk. The bulky suit restricted his arms and legs, and the magnets on his boots were strong. He had to try twice to lift his foot, and he had to lift it extra high to get beyond the pull of the magnetic force. It was weird and uncomfortable, and he had to concentrate just to put one foot in front of the other.

In a strange way it reminded him of the time he had gone hiking in the mountains in camp. He'd been only a little kid and his bunk was going on their first overnight. His pack was almost as big as he was and weighed a lot. He'd been small for his age before he'd turned sixteen, but then shot up seven inches in as many months.

He remembered hiking with that pack, feeling so tired that he could hardly move. And then the rain came down and the path turned to mud, and the mud sucked at his sneakers and held on. It was hard to get his feet out of the ooze. Every step took concentration.

He felt just like that now. He was looking at his feet, ignoring the glory around him, ignoring his companions as well. All he could think about was the next step, getting his foot free

46

from the magnetic hold, trying to keep his balance while the universe swung around him.

And so he wasn't watching when Sergei launched off the station and into space.

The first thing Nathan noticed was that his safety line, which was attached to Sergei behind him, went taut. He felt the jerk, really hard, that pulled him up. Everything happened too fast. If he'd had both feet on the hull, maybe there wouldn't have been enough energy to pull the other magnetic boot off the plating, but he had been in the middle of taking one of those awkward steps. He'd been a little off balance so the sudden tug on the line had sent him over and his own mass plus inertia peeled the boot off the hull.

He grabbed for the safety line, not thinking about Alice in front of him. All he knew was that he was cartwheeling through space. The spinning motion fed on itself, and no matter how he held out his arms or tried to kick, it didn't stop. In fact, his own efforts made him spin faster.

And then the line jerked hard again, pulling him around in the opposite direction. He hung over the station upside down, although it didn't feel that way. Over his head he saw Alice standing solidly with both feet on the hull and her hands on the line. Karl was standing next to her, the arms of his bulky

47

space suit over her shoulders, holding her down.

Nathan slowly pulled himself back in hand over hand on the line, and then tugged gently at Sergei. He was glad he couldn't see anyone's face behind the visors. Sergei touched down gently on the hull. Dr. Thompson's grim voice came over their suit speakers. "I think that's all the excitement we can handle today. Back inside."

Chapter Five

It took nearly an hour to get out of the suits. No one spoke. Sergei looked white and badly shaken. No one had ever seen Sergei lose his cool like that. When they were out of the suits and back in the station uniform shorts, they followed Dr. Thompson back out into the pre-airlock. Nathan was certain that they were going to be reprimanded yet again, although he had no idea what had gone wrong.

But Dr. Thompson didn't yell at them. Instead, he held up the end of the safety cable, a thin twist of super-strong titanium wire around a welded ring. The ring should have been attached to the lock. But it was loose in Dr. Thompson's hands. He held it and studied it as if he had never seen anything like it before.

"What happened, Sergei?" he asked mildly.

Sergei took a deep, ragged breath. "I don't know. One minute I was trying to take a step, and the next I was blasted off the hull. I didn't do anything. I didn't jump, really."

Dr. Thompson nodded absently. "I believe you," he said calmly, twisting the ring in his hands.

"Do you think that someone wants to sabotage the program? Or just us?" Karl asked.

"I don't know what it means," Dr. Thompson said slowly, choosing his words carefully. "But I can't believe that someone out here would try to hurt us. Everyone is too carefully screened, and everyone cares too much about the success of any space mission to sabotage it. No, I think that something triggered the emergency escape explosives on the hatch. They're supposed to be there in case someone is outside and in danger, so they aren't tied to the hull and strangled or something. The electronics are very delicate. But since this isn't Earth, there aren't any radiophones and shortwaves to set them off accidentally. I just don't know."

He looked up at them and shook his head. "Take the rest of the day off, play some computer games, and rest up. Tomorrow we'll go out the Green airlock. That's far enough from anything and on the dark side of the station too. Green isn't being used for anything yet; there shouldn't be any interference there."

"You mean we're going out again?" Noemi wailed. "After Sergei and Nathan nearly got

50

killed?"

"If we don't go, we'll lose our nerve," Lanie said in a steely voice. "We should go right now, this minute."

Everyone froze and looked at Lanie. Fear filled the small room, fear and determination. No one was going to back out now. Lanie swallowed hard.

"Lanie's right," Karl agreed. "Dr. Thompson, maybe we should begin at once?"

Their supervisor smiled warmly. They had never seen this expression on his face before.

"You kids are all right," Dr. Thompson said approvingly. Then he picked up the intercom to report the accident and request a transfer to the Green air lock.

This time when Nathan stepped out into the vacuum of space he was prepared. The brilliance was still there, but it alternated with stark shadows on the dark side of the station. There was nothing soft or indistinct here, nothing that was at all welcoming to life. Knowing that just on the other side of this suit was extreme cold and vacuum was enough to keep Nathan in awe.

They moved more slowly, and this time it seemed easier. Not because the magnetic attraction was any less, but because they were more used to spacewalking.

51

As the team took careful steps across the station's outer skin, Nathan found himself getting a rhythm and balance. It wasn't too different from his skateboard. Only here he had to balance his force with motion instead of with his weight. Once he understood that, all those hours working on the ramp in Eddie's driveway began to pay off. He was used to counterbalancing motion.

A few steps farther and he found it strangely enjoyable. Now he was good enough so that he didn't have to watch his feet every second and could take a moment to glance up.

From Green position he couldn't see the solar sail, but he could see the construction of the colony ships under way in the distance. They were sleek skeletons dangling wires and fine equipment in the void. Nathan was surprised that such delicate machinery had been left out to the elements—until he remembered that there were no elements.

Here he was, Nathan Long, standing with his head hanging toward the sun, nothing but 93 million miles (give or take a few) between him and a real living, flaming star. He wanted to pinch himself to make sure he was awake, but the bulky pressure suit was in the way.

After half an hour Dr. Thompson led them back through the Green air lock. They went through the entire hour-long drill to take off the

52

pressure suits, check them over, and replace the air in the tanks.

"No matter what, do not forget to replace the air in your tanks," Dr. Thompson said firmly. "Never leave it for later. Every tank on the rack should be full at all times. And of course you always check it when you are ready to use it again. Running out of air is the fastest way to die out here."

"Well, at least we don't have to worry about car crashes," Lanie joked. Then she remembered that Karl had lost his mother in a highway accident just a little over a year ago. "Whoops—sorry," she mumbled, turning deep red.

Karl shrugged and turned away. Lanie tried to toss her head in the old Lanie way, to show that she was too tough to care, but it didn't feel the same anymore. She wanted to shrink into the wall, anything at all to get away.

"Hey, you guys, in case you hadn't noticed, dinner is half over," Gen announced. "If we want anything besides leftover tuna surprise, we'd better move."

After dinner they went back to Yellow D. It had become the unofficial To Mars Together hangout. Someone had lettered the logo in the five official languages of the U.N., and inside someone with a bad sense of humor had put up travel posters. Karl had rigged the sound system and Gen had generously offered his disks for general listening. He was hurt when no one seemed interested.

Gen still seemed a little morose. Now he was playing chess with Karl on the magnetic set that kept the pieces in place—which was strange, Nathan thought, considering that chess wasn't exactly Gen's favorite pastime.

Yellow D was home to all the different teams, more comfortable than any other place on the station. After dinner even Suki Long and Anders were there playing zero-G Ping-Pong, which was the sort of weird game that the supervisors didn't approve of.

Nathan saw her and gave a half wave. He disliked Suki Long more than any other person on the program, and maybe more than any other person he had ever met in his life. Just because they had the same last name they had become rivals, and her stuck-up behavior made him sick. He would have ignored her, except he didn't want her to feel special in any way. Pretending that she was just like everyone else was the best he could do.

He was surprised when she handed her paddle to her teammate Anders and pushed herself across the room to meet him. She didn't use the Velcro wristband, just hung on to the support strut with her fingers.

"Sorry about that little accident your team had," she said. "Trouble certainly does follow you guys around. What happened, your juvenile delinquent too good at picking locks?"

Nathan had never wanted to punch a girl in the face before. He wanted to now.

"You're one to talk," Lisette said, saving Nathan from having to respond. "Even in Geneva we heard about your team on the survival trek. How you left your own teammates and stole a car and then wrecked it. If anyone's a delinquent, you are!"

Suki saw everyone was staring at her. "Why don't you mind your own business!" she hissed. "I wasn't talking to you." Then she moved away, trying to pretend she was above them all anyway.

Nathan grinned at Lisette. She really was cute, with fair skin and eyes so dark and soft they made him think of Hershey's syrup. All the girls in the program were smart, and a good number of them were pretty, but Lisette was almost as down-to-earth as Alice without his teammate's seriousness. There was a hint of mischief and fun in those huge chocolate eyes.

"It's a good thing you spoke up," Nathan said gratefully. "I was ready to strangle her."

Lisette grinned back. "Yeah. It showed. Remind me never to get on your bad side."

Nathan wondered if he should ask her on a

date. But what could they do on a date aboard a space station? he thought.

"Hey, now that Suki's gone, the Ping-Pong set is free," he said a little lamely. "You up for a game?"

"I would like to," she answered. "Really. But I've been thinking about your little accident all during dinner. You see, I was on a terminal when it happened, and I noticed a power surge on-screen. I need to talk to Dr. Thompson."

"I'll go with you," Nathan offered.

He hadn't noticed that Sergei had come in and was giving Lisette a funny look.

"Why don't we all go," Sergei suggested.

"He's in Blue Seven-Seven-Two," Lanie said, still glued to her computer screen.

"How'd you know that?" Noemi asked.

Lanie looked up. "I'm psychic," she answered deadpan. She waited for them to laugh, and there was a moment before anyone got the joke. "Okay, I just put a trace on his log-on code. He happens to be on the system, and he's checked into a terminal. I figured I'd better get the trace going before you goons got us lost.'"

Gen led the way. Having once looked at the station schematic, he had instantly memorized the location of every room and cubbyhole, and he led with confidence. They had never been to the Blue level before, but when they got there, they found it exactly like Red and Orange and

Yellow. All the rooms and segments, the facilities, gyms, and lounges were in the same place. But where there were dorms on Red and Orange and classrooms and labs on Yellow, there was a series of offices and workstations on Blue.

The office where Dr. Thompson was working wasn't an office at all. It was a cubby set back from the corridor, one of a set of fifty that lined the walls in this area. Obviously this was computer central. Lanie looked at all the equipment. She bet that any one of the hookups she was looking at had more access than her usual terminal in the Yellow lounge.

"I'm doing the talking," Lisette said firmly.

Nathan nodded.

"Dr. Thompson," she said softly. "Excuse me, but I'd been wondering about something. There was a power surge on the line today, and I was wondering if you knew about a malfunction in the equipment that might have caused it."

The supervisor turned around slowly. He faced Lisette, and then saw the rest of them waiting. "I see," he said carefully. "You're curious about the accident, aren't you? So am I. That shouldn't have happened. I've gone through all the records and I don't have a clue."

"Weird," Lanie said.

"Definitely weird," Gen agreed.

"You know," Dr. Thompson said, "that power surge could be a good place to start your new project."

"What new project," Noemi groaned.

"Something special to suit your individual skills. And I think I'm going to put you all to work on this electrical current problem. Not that we won't be working on it too, but I think a little investigation will do you all good. Keep your minds occupied with something useful for a change."

"What about my team?" Lisette demanded. "What can we do?"

Dr. Thompson held up his hand. "I'm getting to that, if you'll give me a chance. Your team will take care of questioning people. I don't want Nathan's team talking to people they've had so many problems with before. Your team can approach them more easily. Lisette, you and your team have the human angle. Nathan, your team has the technical side of things, how it was all done."

Karl was already rubbing his hands in glee.

"We'll need all the available data," Noemi said.

Sergei was looking at Lisette in a way Nathan didn't like. "I can give you one really good place to start," he suggested. "And I'd be happy to help you out, since you don't know Suki Long and I do. We'd do a great job together."

"You think Suki Long is responsible?" Lisette asked.

Sergei shrugged. "She's the kind of person who might do a thing like that. Don't you think so? Why don't we discuss it over a snack? I saw a whole stash of chocolate down in Yellow kitchen. Interested?"

"C'mon, Sergei, cut it out! This is serious business," Nathan said, his face turning slightly red with annoyance.

"All in the interest of science, my friend," Sergei said.

Somehow, Nathan didn't believe him.

Chapter Six

Two days later the investigation was a big fat nowhere. But that wasn't the thing that bothered Nathan the most. He wasn't even as upset by the fact that there had been another strange electrical surge in the new construction, one that had knocked out some of the stored programs from the computer. He had real problems with Sergei and Lisette.

They were back in Yellow D, getting ready for their Galileo orientation in Blue section. Galileo was the orbital radio telescope launched in the 1980s, one of the longest-lived efforts at international cooperation in space. The telescope, unaffected by Earth's atmosphere, could detect finer signals than anything before and had contributed huge amounts of data to astronomical research.

This should have been one of the most interesting parts of their sojourn aboard *Icarus*.

Until two days ago Nathan had been looking forward to it with real pleasure. He had never dreamed of having a chance to get this close a "look" at the stars, and he wasn't about to waste it.

Everyone in the team was in the lounge. Karl was at his chess game with Gen, the one activity the two of them shared without argument. Lanie was in her usual place at the terminal, and Alice was playing Ping-Pong, the zero-G version with the soft Velcro ball. Noemi was anchored in the corner avidly filing her nails, her heirloom diamond necklace glittering on her program T-shirt. Everyone was there except Sergei. Nathan had a good idea where Sergei was, and it didn't improve his mood.

"You know, that's really stupid, wearing a fortune in diamonds here," Nathan snapped at Noemi. "Why don't you lock them up, where they belong?"

Noemi looked up, her round eyes filling with tears. Alice signaled to her partner and put down her paddle. "You don't have to pick on Noemi too."

But Noemi was already sobbing. "There's nothing nice here at all. Nothing pretty, nothing that isn't functional and ugly and plain."

"Well, did you think there were going to be shopping malls on Mars?" Nathan answered.

"Hey, dude, chill out," Gen said, looking up

from the magnetic chess set. "Lay off her. Lay off the rest of us too, okay? If you're angry at Sergei, why don't you take it up with him? This isn't like you, man."

Nathan blinked rapidly, brought back to reality. It had happed more than once in the past couple of days. The anger had built and built inside him and just tore out at the first available target. It wasn't like him, and seeing Noemi so miserable made him really sorry. He muttered a heartfelt apology to Noemi, and hugged her as though she were the little sister he never had. But he knew that wasn't enough. Nothing could make the words he had said disappear.

Worse than that, much as he was angry at Sergei, there was nothing he could say. Sergei hadn't done anything wrong, and he'd always known the Russian had an eye for girls. Besides, Sergei looked like a teen movie star and all the girls were crazy about him. It wasn't his fault if he was born with perfect features, piercing blue eyes, and a smile that was made to do toothpaste ads.

And it wasn't as if Lisette were Nathan's girlfriend either. Sergei was too good a friend to steal his girl. At least Nathan hoped so. But he didn't have any claim on the Canadian girl at all. Only he liked her so much and it felt like poison in his gut to think of Sergei with her all the time. He didn't have a prayer.

Looking at Noemi's tear-streaked face, Nathan was suddenly scared. He always thought he was an easygoing guy, maybe with a bit of an attitude but loyal to his friends. Now he'd gone and hurt Noemi and for no reason at all. He was afraid that the jealousy was more than he could control, and that it was in charge of him. It sure had worked that way for the past forty-eight hours.

"There isn't any reason for it to be so ugly," Noemi was going on. "The stars are beautiful. We have the most gorgeous view in the whole universe. And all the time we're cramped into these tiny little rooms without any comfort at all. It would be nice if there were some soft carpeting to push off of, and it could be a nice color too. I mean, yellow is nice, but they chose the ugliest shade in the whole paint catalog."

"That's because it was approved by a government committee and someone bought the cheapest stuff," Karl said.

"Or some factory had a surplus. It's easy to imagine why they'd have a surplus of this color," Sergei said from the doorway.

Nathan whipped around. He had no idea how long Sergei had been there. It couldn't have been very long though. At least he hoped not. Lashing out at Noemi was bad enough without Sergei seeing him.

Noting the Russian's arrival, Nathan immediately searched for Lisette. At least he could look at her, ask her about her side of the investigation, get a conversation going. He could show her that he had something to offer too. But she was nowhere to be seen.

"Well, why are we hanging around here?" Sergei asked. "Aren't we supposed to be in Blue Two-G for our Galileo orientation? Come on, this is the part I've been dying for."

"We were waiting for you," Nathan said dryly. "Now that we're all here, we'd better get going. Unless you want to explain why we're late."

The Galileo wasn't exactly a telescope, Dr. Thompson explained. It was a radio antenna picking up vibrations of energy that the eye could not see. These pictures of the "radio universe" showed things that no one had ever expected. The instrument could even pick up the background radiation that scientists thought was the echo of the "big bang," trillions of years ago.

"We've already done studies of the planets of our own solar system," Dr. Thompson said. "In fact, some of the data we have about Mars came from this office. Now we're studying the distant galaxies to understand their structure.

And later on this year, the International Solar Studies Institute will do an intensive analysis of our own sun."

"What's so interesting about our own sun?" Karl asked, baffled.

Dr. Thompson shook his head. "Our sun happens to be the nearest available star to study. And there's a lot we don't know about stars, including our own sun. We still don't understand sun spots, solar storms, flares. All kinds of things are happening in there, and the more we know about our local star, the more we know about stars in general.

"For example, the really strange stuff — black holes and quasars and neutron stars — they're formed when a normal star like our sun dies. It uses up all its fuel and then collapses on itself. If the star is normal size like our sun, it becomes a white dwarf. But if it's a large star, then it explodes in a nova and collapses down even smaller, with all that mass pressed into a tiny area. Some neutron stars are only ten miles in diameter. But their matter is so condensed that a teaspoonful would weigh hundreds of tons."

He showed them pictures of stars taken with Galileo, things that showed strange energy maps. Nathan remembered a picture of Earth he had seen once, taken so that the magnetic fields showed like bright loops above the atmosphere. And there were always the beautiful pictures of the corona of the sun, taken during eclipses. The universe was a strange and beautiful place. But dangerous.

"Anyway, the astronomy sector of the project here has invited all of you to come down whenever you want, so long as you clear it with me first. We love to share our work with everyone who's interested." Dr. Thompson's face absolutely glowed. He was talking from his own love now, his own conviction. He might be one hard-nosed supervisor, but Nathan remembered that he was also the project's astronaut-physicist. He bet that was more like *astro*physicist. He would put real money on it. Then he remembered that he didn't have real money. He probably wouldn't have any for a long time. The thought startled him, and it was a little scary besides.

It wasn't the big things that were hard. He'd thought for a long time about leaving his mother alone, about his friends, and even his school. There was a lot of normal life he was giving up, a lot of things he'd looked forward to. He had decided that this adventure was worth the price and had faced the fact that he was putting his life on hold for at least three years before he would be able to return home.

What surprised him were the little things. Like missing pizza or french fries or the latest issue of *X-Man*. That there was no MTV in space, no swimsuit edition of *Sports Illustrated,* and no football.

On the other hand, there were also no grades and more video games than he had ever imagined. And they were all free too. And there was weightlessness, the most wonderfully free feeling that existed. Definitely the benefits were heavy odds. And three years was *that* long anyway?

Nathan was so caught up in his own ideas that he forgot to be angry at Sergei. He looked at the pictures, watched the demonstration, and signed up for a time to visit on his own, when he would get to go over any of the data that interested him in particular. He found himself signed up with Sergei for the viewing of M-31, a distant galaxy that was the only one that could be seen from Earth with the naked eye.

But he was going to have to deal with Sergei and his competition over Lisette real soon. There was no way they could survive without some understanding. Nathan felt like he was going to explode.

"We can pick up distant galaxies, but we can't get MTV," Gen muttered. Nathan turned to the Japanese boy and studied him. Nathan had thought Gen's bad mood was because of some disagreement with Karl, which was usual. He'd never considered something like this.

"That's really eating at you?" he asked, more than a little incredulous.

"Yeah," Gen admitted. "I feel out of touch with my music, you know. New albums and stuff. Did they expect us to go to Mars and live without music?"

Nathan thought about that one. It did seem a little extreme. And there was the fact that *Icarus* was more than able to handle the transmissions despite the five-hour difference between it and Earth. Well, it might be worth a shot.

A smile spread slowly over his features as the plan formed. Not just for Gen, but for Lisette as well. And for everyone. There wasn't a single program member who didn't like music. Well, there was one. Suki Long. He was certain that she would have a fit, and it would be worth doing just to watch her blow up in little bits.

"It's an interesting problem," Karl admitted grudgingly. "After all, we'd be trying to adjust the receptors on *Icarus* to receive satellite broadcasts from Earth. Tricky."

"Don't tell me why we can't do it, Karl," Nathan said. "Let's figure out a way we can."

"Just to make Gen feel better?" Karl asked sourly.

"No," Alice said. She had been playing a

game of Ping-Pong with Lanie and winning. "It's for everyone. We're too cramped up here, and there's too much to do. And the schedule is too tight for any time off. We need a mental-health break."

"I'll say," Lanie agreed, hooking the Velcro ball on her wristband. "And once we figure out what needs to be done, doing it won't be that bad."

Nathan looked at her quizzically. He had planned the meeting for a time when Noemi and Gen were attending a seminar for the more mathematically gifted astronauts, adult as well as adolescent. He wanted to surprise Gen, but even more, he didn't want to get the other boy's hopes up too much in case it didn't happen.

"We already got a radio," Sergei suggested. "That's easy."

"That's garbage," Lanie argued. "The most powerful stations are Top Forty, and that would make Gen even worse. Not to mention me. No, we're going for something that Dr. Thompson doesn't have in his collection or you can count me out."

"We'll have to consider our alternatives," Alice announced. Then she turned to Lanie. "That's my serve, I think. And we're seven to two, if I'm not mistaken."

Lanie rolled her eyes. She might be able to

make a computer jump through hoops, but she couldn't make a Ping-Pong ball go into the right part of the room, let alone the scoring zone marked on the opposite wall.

Chapter Seven

It was their second time out on the welding crew. The work was hard, awkward in the stiff, bulky suits, but Nathan didn't care. The huge cigar-shaped hulk of the *Santa Maria* was taking shape under him at a rate faster than he had ever imagined. His own work and others' had made a difference in creating the ship that would take them to Mars.

In the vacuum of space, the arc welders flared and sputtered. Nathan held on to his end of a plate, using a wrench to fix the bolts in place. It was difficult to feel the wrench through his thick gloves, to know when he had the bolt down hard enough to squeeze the soft solder. But not so hard that he snapped off the head of the bolt, which he had already done twice this crew period.

Lanie was on the other end of the plate and Gen was holding the torch with Noemi beside him, keeping the air feed going. Strange to think that without oxygen, fire couldn't burn, and there couldn't be a fire in a vacuum. On the other hand, it made the environment so much more dangerous. With an oxygen-rich mixture inside *Icarus,* it meant that if there were a fire, it would travel much faster and burn much hotter.

Nathan was concentrating on his bolt when he realized that the torch had gone out. Noemi, he thought with displeasure. She was probably thinking about some theorem and just forgot the feed.

Nathan watched Noemi and Gen tethered to the supporting strut, trying to make adjustments. No sparks came out of the torch. Maybe the thing was dead.

He didn't hear anything, though, and that was strange. They should be talking to each other, to anyone. He'd checked his radio before they left. Turning off the radio so they could pretend they didn't know when Dr. Thompson chewed them out was not a very good idea. Not if they wanted to stay alive. But now the radio seemed dead too.

Gen and Noemi hauled themselves up to the strut and leaned their helmets against the long steel pole. Nathan understood and leaned his helmet as well. Sound waves don't travel through a vacuum, but they would travel through the strut. Not great, but better than nothing at all.

"Static," Gen said.

Nathan listened carefully. Gen was right, there was a background of static in the headphones, so undertoned and subtle that he hadn't noticed it at first.

"Let's go," Nathan suggested. The sound wasn't good enough to try more than a few words, and even those weren't clear.

Noemi and Gen came down the strut hand over hand. Even though they were tied, it was better to keep a hand on something solid all the time. Just in case. Lanie had turned on her magnetic boots and was shuffling toward them, not removing her feet from the plating. They linked their safety lines together and locked their boots into the sled. Nathan pressed the oversized green ignition button. Again, nothing.

They looked at each other through the deeply tinted faceplates. Nathan was glad that no one could see the panic rising in him. They were stranded. Without the sled there was no way they could get back to *Icarus* and safety. Unless they climbed all around the outer hull of the *Santa Maria*. That would most likely exhaust their oxygen supply. Hard climbing took more air than simply using a wrench and a welding torch.

Then Gen leaned forward. That was easier. With their helmets touching they could talk almost as well as they could in atmosphere.

"We've got to get back," Lanie said sharply.

"Don't waste air saying what everybody knows. Either make a suggestion or be quiet," Nathan ordered.

There was a long moment of silence. Then Noemi held up the tank she'd been using to feed the fire. "But how do we get it in the sled tanks?" she asked.

Lanie inspected the nozzle on the tank, then the connections on the back of Gen's pack. She made a thumbs-down gesture. No fit.

"Balloon," Gen said, pointing to Noemi's extra tank.

Nathan smiled and gave Gen the thumbs-up. While Lanie and Gen used their safety lines to secure the tank into the exposed steering bands of the sled, Nathan took the wheel. The power used generally came from the pair of thrusters in the rear, but they managed to wedge the tank between the bands in the back. Well, they were able to once Lanie had pried the fancy thruster out of its mount. Then Noemi turned on the gas. At the first whoosh of thrust the sled headed straight for *Icarus,* only a kilometer away.

The power from the compressed oxygen was almost as strong as the thrust from the microjets on the sled. They were making good headway. Noemi worked the nozzle just as she had for Gen's welding and Nathan steered. The sled approached *Icarus* at full tilt, just as the air in the welding tank ran out.

But the sled kept going at full speed. There was no friction to slow them down. Eventually they would lose energy, but without thrust, they didn't have any control over steering. All they had was a runaway sled, and it looked like they were heading straight for the hull of *Icarus.*

Time slowed down for Nathan, and he wasn't afraid anymore. He knew how dangerous their situation was, and yet he felt strangely detached, as if he were watching it all in a movie. Very deliberately he removed his safety harness. *Icarus* was growing closer by the moment.

He touched his helmet to the others. "Just pretend it's Yellow D," he said quietly. "Push the sled away so it doesn't tear the station skin. And then use the momentum to push

75

toward the station, boots first with the magnets on."

He didn't wait for the others to agree. He released the lock on his own boots, pointed at the approaching hull of the station, and used his fingers to count. One, two, three.

Then he crouched, pushed, spun around, and heard his feet lock solidly on the station hull. It was just like Yellow D. It had almost been too easy.

He looked around. Yes, there was Gen and Lanie, and even Noemi had made it just fine. With the magnets on their boots, Nathan hooked his safety line to Lanie, then she hooked on to Noemi and Gen was at the end.

Nathan led them cautiously through the metal landscape. He didn't know where he was. There were no markings on the outside of the station, no colors, and he didn't know where the air lock was. But there had to be one close by. Somewhere.

It was bright, so bright that he had the extra protective shield down over his faceplate. Nathan stopped for a moment and tried to remember the curvature of the station, hoping that would give him a clue. He wished Alice were with them. She was good at working out directions.

And then he felt a firm tug at his safety

line. His eyes jerked up, frightened. If Lanie had floated off . . . But Lanie was signaling to him, pointing to Gen.

Gen was pointing to a distant dark spot on the hull. Of course, Gen remembered from their one time out. That crazy memory of his. Nathan gestured to Gen to take the lead. The four of them shuffled off to the air lock, not fifteen meters away.

The real fear didn't hit until later. Somehow Nathan managed to get out of his pressure suit, check it through the rack, and refill his air tanks without noticing how he had done it. Then he had put on his favorite shorts, the blue ones with the black skulls and spiders printed on them, and his blue Billy Bong shirt, and walked out of the changing area as if he were fine.

But when he saw Gen hanging by his heels, his eyes closed, breathing deeply, Nathan suddenly acknowledged how close they'd been to death. His heart started to race and his stomach balled up. He swallowed hard, afraid that he would throw up right there in the corridor.

Fear was cold, followed by hot anger. Who had done that to them? Because that wasn't just a stunt the way draining the battery in

Gen's land vehicle had been during the survival trek back in Houston. That could have only hurt them. This could have killed them.

Nathan imagined Suki Long's sneering, contemptuous face and pounded his fist into the palm of his hand. Gen's eyes flew open.

"Let it go, dude," Gen said softly, as if he were very far away. "Just let it go. We're here, we're safe. Close your eyes and pretend that it was a bad dream. Like we've never really left *Icarus* and everything is okay."

Nathan swallowed hard again, trying to capture the fear and the anger together and force them back down. He just wanted to get still, to get steady.

"We've got to stop it," Nathan said after a long moment passed. "The investigation is key, and I can't just let Sergei play around with Lisette and call that doing something. We almost got killed out there, and we'd better not forget it. We'd better be real clear that pranks in space are deadly."

"I don't think it was a prank," Lanie said from behind him.

Nathan whipped around so fast that he started to spin, and had to throw out a Velcroed wrist to stabilize himself. "What?" he asked, once he had gotten steady.

There was something about the two girls

78

coming out just then that made the horror of the past hour fade. Noemi was wearing her diamonds with a soft oversized shirt that was kept in place by lime-green suspenders on her shorts. Somehow she managed to look completely silly and chic at the same time. Nathan almost wanted to laugh.

Lanie was another story. With her soft blond hair shorter and wearing a faded black tank top with the words "Harley-Davidson" surrounded by pink roses, she looked more like she was trying to be tougher than she really was.

"Look at what happened. The radios went out, the torch went out, the ignition switch in the sled went out. But the boots still worked and the spray nozzle on the air tank still worked. It was only the electronics that malfunctioned, and everything else worked fine."

"So why is that not a prank?" Gen asked, his interest as much intellectual as practical.

"Because if someone played a prank and messed up the sled, they would have done something easier than the ignition switch. But that's not all. How would anyone mess up the torch, and our suit radios? The torches are stored in the engineering section and we don't get near them until they're passed out during a crew shift. Or some other crew is using them before us. But there's no way to know that one torch is going to one group, right?"

She paused to let her reasoning sink in. Then she continued. "But the biggest thing is the suit radios. The way those suits are made, if anyone had tampered, they would have to rip the foam lining out to get to the headset, and then reglue it. That would show, and we'd feel it too. Because if you reglue the lining it feels funny and doesn't fit exactly right anymore."

"Really?" Noemi asked, her eyes huge.

Lanie nodded. "Believe me. I found out the hard way on a motorcycle helmet. But that's not the only thing. They all went out at the same time."

She didn't say anything else. The idea sank in slowly. This was no prank. But maybe it was a conspiracy.

"Electrical interference," Gen said softly, his eyes slightly glazed. "It has to be interference. Only who would do something like that? It would affect everyone working outside *Icarus*. For all we know, it would affect *Icarus* too."

"An electromagnetic pulse would do it," Nathan said, his throat so dry that he could barely get the words out. "Which would mean some sort of nuclear explosion."

"If that was it, we'd all be dead. But just

to make sure, let's ask," Lanie said decisively. She jabbed the intercom. "Hey, anyone, was there any kind of explosion out there in the past hour?"

That was a stupid way to ask, and aloud the question seemed absurd. But there was nothing else Nathan could think of, nothing at all.

"No," a voice said through the intercom, sounding totally confused. "No explosions of any kind. Why?"

But Lanie flicked off the intercom and shrugged. "Let's go," she said.

Nathan didn't follow her back to Yellow D. Instead, he went to the dorm, which was empty at this time of day. He needed to catch his breath and think.

An electronic interruption. And apart from the electromagnetic pulse that followed a nuclear explosion, he didn't know how such a thing could be explained. Everything was happening too fast. Nathan needed a little time to recover. He pulled out his own portable disk player and went through his CD selection. Nothing was right.

Feeling a little guilty, although Gen said he was welcome anytime, he looked through Gen's. There was an Iron Maiden album, all about days when battles were done with

81

swords and wooden ships had sailed the oceans. That was far enough away from any reality he knew. As he pressed the play button he relaxed and thought of home.

Chapter Eight

They already had their ship assignments. The list had come through that morning, but Lanie had gone in and pirated a copy the night before. None of them could wait to find out which ship they were on and if certain people were going with them.

"I hope Raisa isn't with us," Sergei had whispered as they waited in the abandoned Blue corridor for Lanie to finish at the terminal cubby. "If Raisa finds out about Lisette and Ludmilla, then I'm in trouble. I promised both Raisa and Ludmilla that I would be their boyfriend on Mars," he confided to Gen.

"You are too hung up on girls," Gen said, his long hair shaking from side to side like seaweed floating without gravity. "The only person I don't want on that ship with us is

Suki Long."

Nathan had laughed in agreement as well as nervousness. He was certain that someone would come around the turn in the corridor any minute and report them. It had struck him as very odd that they had been able to get into the Blue terminals so easily in the first place.

"Well, it's easier than breaking into a locked office," Lanie had reminded him. They had done that in Houston when their team had been posted at the bottom of the selection group at the midtrial period. She had gone into the system then to find out if there had been a mistake, or if someone had tampered with their standing.

She had found that the record was correct. It wasn't until much later that Dr. Thompson had explained that the list had been inverted to see how the candidates would react. The Mars program couldn't tolerate any quitters. Mars was going to be tough no matter how good they were, no matter how much backup they had going. People who fell apart under pressure just wouldn't cut it as pioneers.

But here on *Icarus* there were no locks, there were no offices, there was nothing to keep them out at all. Once Lanie had discovered the layered access terminals down on

Blue, she had compiled a codeword directory immediately. And there was nothing at all to keep her out, as if no one had ever anticipated the possibility that a person might not have the purest motives in logging on.

"No challenge at all," Lanie had grumbled.

Karl had crossed his eyes, which had made Alice giggle. "Just let the computer stuff be a challenge," he said. "You're already expert at breaking and entering."

Lanie looked as if she were about to deck him. Karl smirked, goading her on, and Lanie swung hard.

On Earth her punch might have knocked out a couple of teeth. Here, weightless, Newton took over. For every action there is an equal and opposite reaction. Lanie's swing forward took all her strength and propelled her backward just as hard. She'd barely touched Karl, but slammed herself hard into the wall behind her, and yelled when she hit.

"The laws of physics are not about to be broken, even if you've already broken all the rest," Karl said triumphantly.

Lanie only hissed.

Nathan wanted to pound both their heads into the hull. He thought they'd gotten over the worst of their mutual dislike. Now they were fighting again. Nathan knew that Karl resented how talented Lanie was with a computer every bit as much as he was horrified by her checkered past. Well, she couldn't help it if life in the projects had required some specialized skills. And she was trying. Karl wasn't.

"Okay, the two of you," Nathan said. "Either we're doing this or we're not. But we're not going to hang around here and fight about it, understand? Whoever makes the next crack, I'm personally going to report to Dr. Thompson."

That had shut both of them up, at least long enough for Lanie to identify the high-access terminal and get past the first layers of code. She had to get deep into the data base to find the duty rosters.

"Well, I found it," Lanie exclaimed. "You want to know or not?"

"Tell," Nathan said impatiently.

"We're all on the *Santa Maria*," Lanie said.

"What about Ludmilla and Raisa?" Sergei asked.

"What about Lisette?" Nathan interrupted.

Lanie rolled her eyes and went back to the screen. "It'd be a whole lot easier with last names, you know," she muttered. "Well, here it is. There's a Ludmilla on the *Nina* and a Raisa on the *Pinta*. And Lisette is on the

Santa Maria with us."

"What about Suki?" Alice asked.

"I know she's going to be with us," Sergei moaned. "We can't escape fate — or Suki Long."

But Lanie was shaking her head. "She's on the *Nina*. So you can stop sounding like a dying donkey, Sergei."

"I'll bet you never even saw a donkey in your life," Sergei shot back. "I'll bet you never heard one, healthy or dying, or a mule or a cow or a . . ."

"But she was right," Alice pointed out. "And I've heard plenty of donkeys and sheep and all kinds of animals. And you, Sergei, Mr. City-Boy, if you don't stop, someone'll be here just to get you to sick bay."

Sergei smiled. "That's what I love about you, Alice. You're always so much fun."

It was much later when Alice came up with the perfect way to get the music videos for Gen. She had gotten hold of Nathan and Sergei after dinner while Gen was in the dorm lost in his headphones and Lanie was trying to fix the fifth level on one of the games.

"Do you remember that we're supposed to communicate with other members of the pro-

87

ject who didn't make the final cut?" she asked carefully. "That we're supposed to do weekly reports? And it's my turn on Thursday."

Nathan nodded, and missed the ball. Sergei scored and Nathan scowled at him. Sergei was a little too obnoxious these days, and the matter with Lisette still wasn't resolved.

Alice snorted and missed, so Nathan was at least able to even up the point average. "I can ask whoever is on the other end to tape the show Gen likes and then send it out in a dense signal, which we can intercept and then record and play back whenever we want. And all we have to do is change the broadcast computer log."

Sergei whistled through his teeth. "Excellent. I wish I'd thought of it myself."

Alice smiled gamely. "I wish I had too. But it was really Lanie, Noemi, and Lisette. I just pointed out that we had an opportunity to make contact with a sympathetic party."

"Lisette?" Nathan muttered. "What does she know about this?"

Sergei turned red and stuck the Velcro paddle to the strut in defeat. "I was just talking to her," he said defensively. "It wasn't like we'd agreed it was secret. But she's very good at things and I thought she might be able to help. And she was."

Nathan could feel the anger again. Sergei was his friend. They'd been through more together than he'd been through with Eddie back home. Sergei was on his side, at his back. They were buddies in every way that counted. He couldn't let some dark-eyed girl get in the way of that.

But he couldn't help it, he was jealous. There were plenty of pretty girls, why couldn't Sergei choose one of them? Why did he have to pick the one Nathan liked? He had a Russian girlfriend too.

"It's a great idea," Alice repeated. "Simple and easy."

Nathan wanted to say no way. No way at all. They should drop the whole thing. They should just shut up and get on with their work. And most of all, they shouldn't talk about team stuff with outsiders. Especially when the outsider was Lisette and it was Sergei doing the talking.

He was ready to call the whole thing off when Gen showed up, looking just a little out of it, which was usual these days.

"I thought you were listening to music," Sergei said quickly.

Gen just shrugged. "Yeah. But they're all out of date now. It's been weeks. I wonder if the new Skulls and Crystals album is out yet.

Anyway, that wasn't why I was looking for you guys. I just wanted to know if anyone was going to Dr. Thompson's talk on magnetic fields. It sounds interesting."

Nathan blinked fast. "I was planning on it," he lied. He hadn't known there was anything going on, but then, he didn't keep up with what the supervisor was doing. He had even spent less time in the astronomy sector than he had originally hoped because Dr. Thompson was always there.

"You know, Gen, if you go, then you can just tell the rest of us what it was about," Alice said, smiling. "And that way we could avoid Mr. Mean himself."

Gen grinned quickly. "And you wouldn't get caught falling asleep on him."

"No, what she really means is that we can get rid of you long enough to plan a surprise party," Sergei said blandly.

Gen blinked quickly, then laughed so hard that he was pushed backward across the lounge. "That's a scream," he said when he got under control. "That's a riot. You know, you sure are one completely perfect straight man, Sergei."

"No way," Sergei protested. "Karl's the straight man."

And they laughed again.

Alice had gotten through to their capcom, a boy from Indonesia who had almost the same taste as Gen. He had promised to tape *Headbanger's Ball* and send it up in the next broadcast communication.

Lanie got to a Blue access terminal and pulled their special broadcast out before the *Icarus*'s communications office went through the incoming file and routed data and messages to the correct parties. It was all very delicate, even more so because Lanie didn't want to leave a trace in the records.

Much as he had scoffed, Karl looked over Lanie's shoulder as her fingers flew over the keyboard. Nathan could hardly read the first two lines of code before something shimmered on the monitor and Lanie had gone on.

The minutes dragged on. Every flicker of the red chrono in the corner of the screen made Nathan nervous. They were going to be found out and sent back. Someone had already been sent back on a shuttle flight to Earth, someone he hadn't known who had been in the Calcutta selection group. If Thompson got wind of what they were doing, he would be back on Earth before he knew what had hit him.

But Thompson was too busy with this investigation and hadn't been wandering around waiting to catch them. It was all very strange, and somehow Nathan thought that was more important than the demerits or even the risk of being sent home.

"Okay, I've got it," Lanie said. "Let's get out of here."

"But where is it?" Sergei asked.

Lanie threw her head back and laughed freely. "I deleted the message and left a hidden program to route it into Gen's chess program as soon as it comes in. When he calls it up, he's got three hours of heavy metal vids."

"And commercials," Sergei said solemnly. "Don't forget the commercials."

That made Lanie laugh, and even Karl cracked a smile.

Chapter Nine

Early the next day, Lisette found Nathan in the bio lab finishing up his required advanced first aid certification. He'd already done all the work and had managed to miss the test periods.

"Why haven't you answered my messages?" she asked.

"Wait a minute," Nathan had replied. He typed a few more words on the keyboard and pressed enter.

"You know, I have to get this done now or Thompson's going to send me back," he groused. "And what messages? I didn't get any messages."

Lisette shook her head, her heavy dark curls fluttering. "You mean you don't check your box?" she asked, incredulous. "We all have electronic mailboxes. I've been using yours for days and you mean you haven't looked."

Nathan turned red. It had honestly never occurred to him to check it. If someone aboard the station wanted him, he was around. He couldn't see the point of using E-mail when finding someone was easier.

"Well, I wanted to talk to you about this investigation thing," she said briskly. "I think we're in the wrong place. I've checked out Suki as much as I could, and it seems like she's minding her own business like a happy little camper. I figured you ought to know. Sergei keeps talking about other people on her old team, but I just don't see it. And I sort of wish Sergei wouldn't spend every minute making up things we have to do when it's obvious that this investigation is just to throw us all off."

"What do you mean, throw us all off?" Nathan asked, amazed. He wasn't sure he was tracking. Lisette wasn't pleased spending every spare moment in Sergei's company? That was news to him.

"I mean, I think there's something else, something that maybe Thompson suspects but doesn't know yet," she said. "I don't know what it is. I was going to check with Lanie

94

about maybe breaking into his personal file and taking a look around, but I didn't think we should do it on our own. We go in as a group or we forget it."

"That's great. I'm glad you want it to be a group effort. But I don't think it's such a good idea. Lanie breaks into other people's files all the time. It's not a good habit."

Lisette snorted and tried to toss her head. Without gravity the effect just wasn't the same, and she began to spin until the tension on her Velcro sock pulled her back.

"Look," she said, trying to recover her dignity, "whatever's out there could kill us. A solar flare could cook us in a flash with radiation, or an ion storm. I want to know what the story is before I go out there again."

Nathan met her gaze. She was right, of course. Those things could kill them. Other things could kill them too, like carelessness, lack of oxygen, or a seal that wasn't quite up to quality. But that didn't change his mind.

"Did you check the next work rotation?" he asked carefully. "Thompson's out on that one too, and if he knows something we don't, then I'm pretty sure that it'll be safe."

Lisette knit her brows and thought about that. "Good enough," she agreed hesitantly.

"For now at least. If anything happens, we'll have to reevaluate it." She turned and pushed lightly, launching herself toward the port.

"Well, I think we should reevaluate in any case," Nathan said, aware that he was making noise only to keep talking to her. "It's not just a matter of what, it's a matter of when too. We don't exactly have all the time in the universe."

Lisette smiled. "I guess we have all we need," she said lightly. Nathan thought he saw another meaning in her words, then dropped it. He didn't like having to fish for answers. And there were too many questions already. "But I suppose you have to finish your quals," the Canadian girl said crisply.

Nathan turned and pretended to be diligently absorbed in what was in front of him on the screen. He pretended that he didn't notice the hiss of the port seal opening, or the gentle thump as she shut the door.

All the words in front of him turned into jelly and ran over the screen. At first Nathan thought it was just his reaction to Lisette, to her seeking him out. Maybe she really did like him after all. Maybe she was too smart to fall for a charmer like Sergei. He wasn't sure he could finish the qualifying segment anyway.

He glanced back at the board. It was still strange, the colors all washed in irregular stripes across the screen. And it wasn't in his head. This was definitely a computer problem of massive proportions.

He hit the keyboard a couple of times, then tried a few functions and "escape" at least three times, and then the colors resolved and Nathan was confronted with one of the more garish MTV graphics to hit yet. Must be a new one; he sure didn't recognize it from home.

Then came the familiar logo and theme for *Headbanger's Ball*. Startled, he tapped the keyboard again, but it wasn't responding. There had to be a system override. It was one thing to get the show for Gen, but feeding it in to the whole station, that was crazy. It was irresponsible. It might even get them sent home.

The familiar veejay came on, mentioned guests and new videos and what was coming up in the next three hours, and then introduced the first vid. Nathan was horrified. He was powerless to turn the thing off. And he hated, absolutely positively hated, the song they were playing. A pretty-boy band playing a song for junior high girls.

"I hope you're having a good time, Gen,"

Nathan muttered as he unhooked his legs from the anchor bar at the terminal. "I hope you really enjoy this before we all go home." At least the terminal had the good sense to obey the "off" switch.

He kicked off out of the lab and through the compartments that made up Green Level, all the bio labs and medical besides. He passed a working group in the med section and recognized Dr. Allen. She turned to one of the computers and logged on. Nathan grabbed a support and held on, waiting to see what showed up on her screen.

No MTV appeared. Instead, it was the standard log-on message. He waited a moment longer while she called up her E-mail, and that looked like ordinary amber lit words. At least it wasn't playing at every terminal, Nathan thought, and tried to take comfort from that. Or someone already got to it and turned it off, which he thought was more likely.

It took a long time to get to Yellow D. Maybe because there was a research team in the chute, maybe because he was so hyped on adrenaline that the rest of the universe had slowed down in comparison. He nearly collided with a rearguard biologist when he launched down the hall. But at last he arrived

98

to hear loud music and louder laughter.

"It's been so long, I'm even enjoying the commercials," Lanie was saying as Nathan entered.

"What the hell is going on?" Nathan growled behind them. Lanie and Gen turned suddenly. Only Alice remained calm.

"Why are you so upset?" she asked. "We said we were keying the tape to Gen's chess program, and we said we were cuing in our own log-on codes."

Nathan's shoulders sagged in relief. So it was only his sign-on that had routed the tape to where he was working. Only their team would ever get it, or even know.

Lanie laughed and Nathan, relieved, joined her. But it was the look on Gen's face that convinced him that they'd done the right thing. Gen stared at the screen like a starving man at a Thanksgiving dinner with all the trimmings. "A new Soundgarden album," he whispered in a voice as hushed as church. "World premiere video from it tonight."

"It's not my style," Alice said briskly, "but I'm glad you're happy."

"Thank you," Gen said sincerely, although he never took his eyes from the screen. "About a million times."

They all watched the next two vids together,

one a pretty hard tune that Nathan thought was okay and another one that was awesome. Lanie gave it a big thumbs-up but Alice rolled her eyes. At least Karl had the good timing to burst in when they were in the middle of yet another commercial. He was so red in the face, Nathan thought he would pop.

"How dare you include me in your insane schemes?" he exploded all over Yellow D. "I was working on a piece with the station orchestra, and all of them, every one, got a full blast of that, that, that . . ."

"Big deal," Lanie said, baiting him. "So you don't like Gen's music. Okay. We all know that, we all understand. I don't like onions, but I don't bother you about eating them, do I? Even when you microwave them and the smell stinks up the whole kitchen. So if I can tolerate your onions, I don't see why you can't tolerate Gen's music."

The tension between them was as bright as a megawatt flare. They were frozen in time, in an anger that was as much habit as dislike. Lanie hissed like a reptile ready to strike. Karl coiled up, ready to slam himself though space for the maximum impact.

"Yes, I think it's about time," Alice said conversationally. "Don't you, Nathan? They've both been spoiling for a fight for so long, it would be a pity to stop them now."

"Yeah, sure," Nathan agreed quickly, following Alice's lead. She was playing it closer to the edge than Nathan would have liked just then, but it might as well all come at once. He could feel history coalesce around him. "I just figured they waited because Karl didn't want to hit a girl," he added for good measure.

"Possible," Alice agreed cheerily. "If we were betting, who would you bet on? I'm not sure. Lanie is meaner and probably had the experience, but Karl is the best athlete in the whole program. But he might not fight a girl. That makes it hard."

"If you run down both their performance records back in Houston, it's a toss-up," Gen informed them, never taking his eyes from the screen. "I'd give it just about even odds."

"So, if we're betting, what are we betting with?" Nathan asked. "We don't have any money and we don't own anything worth much. I mean, are we talking CDs or T-shirts or what?"

"How about work rotations?" Alice suggested. "You know, the bad ones, like kitchen duty or something else horrible."

Nathan considered and nodded. It took everything in him not to look at either Karl or Lanie. He only hoped that Alice's strategy was working. He'd never have tried it himself. In his opinion both Lanie and Karl were too likely to use their little game as an excuse to hurt each other. But Alice was very good with people, and she knew Lanie far better than he did.

"Do you hear that?" Lanie practically spit out the words. "They're betting on us fighting. I mean, aren't you going to try to stop us?"

"Fighting is clearly against the rules," Karl chimed in. "And I don't want to get sent home. If we were caught, no one would believe that Nathan and Alice deserved it too."

"Yeah," Lanie agreed emphatically. "They're trying to get us in trouble. Well, I'm not going to play their way, okay?"

"Good," Karl said, holding out his hand. "Truce?"

"Truce," Lanie proclaimed, then gently pushed off the wall to meet Karl in the center of Yellow D, where they shook hands with great ceremony. Nathan had to keep himself from cheering. He pantomimed wiping his forehead in relief, and Alice winked back. Gen, completely involved in his *Headbanger's Ball,* didn't notice a thing.

Just when Nathan thought they were finally

102

going to have a little peace, the door to Yellow D opened again. This time it was Noemi, and she looked perfectly miserable. Trailing her like a giant shadow was Dr. Thompson.

"I'm sorry," she said, blowing her nose loudly and hooking the heel of her sock to one of the Velcro pads without looking. "I didn't have any idea of the time, and I was in the Galileo center on my turn to view a pulsar, and I was logged on and then all of a sudden there's this noise and Dr. Thompson is there and he heard it and there wasn't anything I could tell him at all." She paused to get her breath and sob again hysterically.

Karl glared at Nathan and Gen as if it were all their fault. Having recently made a truce with Lanie, she was exempted from his general disapproval.

Dr. Thompson's eyes glowed like red coals. Nathan wondered how anyone could look so demonic. Then he realized that it was the color from the monitor reflected in their supervisor's eyes. But the image was appropriate nevertheless.

"Where's Sergei?" Dr. Thompson asked, his voice deceptively soft.

"Please don't get him," Noemi wailed. "It's finally his turn."

"What's she talking about?" The supervisor

turned to where Nathan and Alice were anchored.

"It's Sergei's turn on kitchen duty," Alice informed him seriously. "And it would be really unfair for him to miss it. We've all gone at least once and he tried to bribe Lanie with a chocolate bar."

"Cheap chocolate," Lanie commented. "Rotten bribe. And I don't do kitchens."

"Neither does Sergei," Alice said pointedly. "He always worms out of it, like he's too good to take his turn with the rest of us. I think he thinks it's the girls' job, no matter what else we can do."

Dr. Thompson listened to them, then silently glided across Yellow D. He was going for the off switch, Nathan was certain. What else would he be doing? But all of a sudden the whole picture and sound collapsed as if they'd been mixed together and put through the food processor.

"What happened?" Gen wailed.

"Electronic interference," Dr. Thompson said, and two deep lines creased his forehead between his eyes. "Again."

Yellow D was as silent as the hard vacuum of space. All of them watched the splatter pattern of static on the screen, frozen for a time that seemed like forever. Each of the team members thought about when they had been outside the station in one of the failures, about how close they had really come to dying. It wasn't pretty.

Chapter Ten

Noemi surprised them. Coolly, with all the right of command and self-possession of the queen of England, the Venezuelan girl faced the screen. "This isn't going to stop us," she said as if she were stating the obvious, not trying to boost anyone's courage. "This isn't going to even slow us down. We have a launch window to make. Besides, we've been up against worse. We had to deal with the competition in Houston and people trying to stab us in the back. A little static isn't even worth the effort."

Just then the static died and was replaced by an interview with a singer Nathan recognized. From the way the singer talked, Nathan figured he had the I.Q. of a turnip.

"But there remains the question of that recording," Dr. Thompson said, recovering himself and sliding smoothly into his role. "That's contraband, unauthorized use of communications facilities, and a few other violations I could name."

But Noemi's speech had stirred Nathan's blood just a little. For a moment he was aware of making a decision, knew that he could be sealing his own travel orders back down to Earth forever. He was perfectly clear that he could be throwing away everything for the sake of a principle.

But if he didn't stand up for himself and his friends, he didn't deserve to go to Mars. If he wimped out, played along with the system like Karl always did, it made him dishonest. This was a fight he could walk away from. But Nathan was tired of walking away, of getting around the rules he could and trying to toe the line so he wouldn't get sent home. He was being totally bogus. And what was worse, he knew it.

He winced, knowing that he was going to take some lumps on this one. Sort of like shooting down the edge of the curb knowing he was going to wipe out and thrilled by it at the same time.

"Then maybe it's time to discuss the rules," Nathan said softly. "We've been hearing a lot about them, what we can do and can't do, in

Houston and here. It's one thing to have rules for safety aboard a space station, that's reasonable. But why should there be a rule against us getting TV we enjoy? What purpose does it serve?" He said the last words very clearly, one at a time.

Noemi had surprised them, but Nathan had blown them away. There was a moment of stunned horror as everyone readjusted to what Nathan meant. He had questioned the very underpinnings of authority in the whole program.

Because there was nothing wrong with watching rock videos, nothing wrong with kitchen raids, nothing wrong with sleeping when they wanted to sleep and eating when they wanted to eat. It was a freedom the adults took for granted.

"It's a matter of discipline, among other things," Dr. Thompson stated stiffly.

Nathan shook his head heavily, as if reluctant to reject the supervisor's position. "Discipline? We do what needs to be done. We report on our work schedule and we're down the line on safety regs. Our reporting quota is higher than in the building group working on the *Santa Maria* right now. You know that. That's discipline. Not being permitted to enjoy simple pleasures because they aren't your pleasures, that's a different matter entirely. Or maybe not. Maybe there are rules forbidding us to request entertainment CDs and stuff because no one ever thought that we'd want anything you didn't already have."

"This is garbage," Dr. Thompson said, gesturing to the screen. "We don't need that here, you don't need it. If you want music, there's a decent CD library in Red Seventeen."

"That's not the point," someone said from behind Dr. Thompson. The tall supervisor turned to face Sergei.

Sergei smiled winningly. Nathan could imagine him flashing the same grin at Lisette, and then shoved the thought firmly aside. For the first time it stayed there, and he didn't feel any of the animosity that had become normal background noise in his life, one of those things he hadn't noticed until it was gone.

"The point is that we are also entitled to a certain amount of communications time, to our personal requests from Earth like everyone else on this station," Sergei said as if reading it out of the rulebook. "Besides which, I don't see how you expect us to colonize a planet while you're telling us when to go to bed and checking to make sure we washed under our fingernails."

Dr. Thompson looked furious. "Well, maybe

109

you'd like to take it up with Dr. Allen," he said. He used his hand to push backward, and didn't turn until he was at the door. It was a show of being a real astronaut. This wasn't his first time in space or on *Icarus*.

Nathan was braced for Karl's expected outburst. At this point it felt like being trapped in an endless video game where the character has to repeat the orders and actions in precise order to advance. Only this was real life.

So it was even more surprising when the outburst didn't come. Karl just hung there, sullen but not speaking, not defending his precious rules and right way of doing things.

"Come on," Nathan said, floating up directly in front of Karl. "Aren't you going to argue?"

Karl waited until Nathan was almost ready to hit him. "I think Sergei does have a point," he said. "Of course, if we all get sent home, it would be your fault."

"Oh, hush up, Karl," Alice chided him. "We don't make or break as a team anymore. They can perfectly well send Nathan home and keep you here, so if you do get sent back, you have no one to blame but yourself."

Alice's pronouncement wasn't so much of a surprise as the fact that they had never noticed. From the first day at Houston they had

110

been told that a team either made the program together or washed out together. Now, though, they had all passed that final hurdle. The only way they could be scrubbed from the mission was to do it alone.

"Well, if Nathan gets sent home for getting me the vid, then I'm going home too," Gen said.

"I don't go to Mars without you guys," Lanie agreed.

And Noemi did it again. "I think we should talk to Dr. Allen. And in the meantime we should make sure that all the others know too. We played it their way for a long time, and now it's time for a compromise. With everyone in the program we negotiate from a position of strength."

Sergei whistled between his teeth. "Where did a rich girl learn Marx?" he asked the walls.

"That's Marx?" Noemi asked completely innocently. "I learned it when Daddy was on the board of the Organization of Oil Producing and Exporting Companies. OPEC raised the price a couple of times, and we had to stand united. When we did, there wasn't anything anyone else could do."

"I didn't know Venezuela was in OPEC," Karl said.

111

"There's a lot you don't know," Lanie added dryly. "Like how about respect. We've been paying dues and now it's time that the powers that be show us a little respect. We've earned it."

"I'll talk to Lisette," Nathan volunteered immediately. "And Vijay and Tara."

"Who's going to talk to Suki?" Sergei asked, his eyes twinkling evilly.

Together Sergei and Nathan turned to Karl and smiled. They looked as if they had rehearsed the whole thing. "You did talk to her before," Sergei reminded him.

"So they can wreck things again?" Gen demanded. He still hadn't quite recovered from Suki's team draining the battery of his vehicle on the survival trek. He had been so proud of that thing and Suki had ruined it. Gen tried not to blame Karl for bragging. After all, Karl was very impressed with Suki and that whole group, and he was just trying to show that his own team had talent. Unfortunately, it had worked out wrong, and Suki had used the information to hurt them.

"No," Karl said slowly. "Maybe we should leave her out of it. Maybe we should just get together the people we know will support us. That should be enough."

112

In the end Lisette spoke to Suki and she never said a word about MTV. The planning meeting was scheduled for Yellow D. Nathan was so nervous, he changed clothes three times. After consideration, he decided on the official red shirt with the To Mars Together logo small and neat over the heart. That made him look more like he represented something, that he was part of the program and proud of it, not trying to go off on his own ego trip.

Each team was sending the leader and one other member. There wasn't enough room in Yellow D for everyone to attend, and besides, they didn't want to alert the adults. Nathan's one other member was Noemi. He would have preferred Sergei or Alice to back him up. Either of them could be counted on to give good solid reasons and make everything sound like it would work.

He was a little worried about Noemi. Everyone knew about her diamonds, and she dressed like Bloomingdale's had a deep-space department. But Alice refused to budge. "It was Noemi's idea and she should be there," Alice had repeated twenty times when they had argued over who should go. "Besides, given her family, maybe she has more experience than we know."

113

Karl had rolled his eyes and Sergei had shrugged and it was decided. Now Nathan was worried that she might show up looking silly in the diamonds and lime-green suspenders. At least she couldn't paint her nails bright pink. That would have been too much.

To his surprise, when he went down to wait in front of the girls dorm, he found Noemi ready and dressed exactly the same as he was. She wasn't wearing any jewelry or makeup, and her thick hair was pulled up in a long clip. Nathan was startled. For a moment he wasn't sure it was the same girl.

Then she giggled. "Alice and Lanie helped," she said. "What do you think?"

"Not even any pink lipstick?" Nathan managed to ask.

Noemi blinked. "Of course not. It wouldn't go with the red."

Somehow the silly typical-Noemi answer made Nathan feel better. They pushed through the corridor to the lift and then down the tube. Amazing how easy it was now to swim weightless through the station. Already he didn't have to think or judge too carefully before he pushed off how much energy to use or how to position his body so that he landed the way he wanted to. It was a lot like learning a new trick on his skateboard. At first it took hours and hours to get the movements right and he had to think about everything. Then, once he got a trick down, it was part of him. His body seemed to know what he was doing all by itself.

He was at home on the space station now. Gravity, his favorite pizza, the feel of cold wind in his face, these things had become hazy memories. Earth itself was in soft focus, the gentle atmosphere itself filtered out the harsh brilliance of space. The memories were strangely distant, almost as if they were someone else's. This was where he belonged for now.

When they got to Yellow D it was full. Noemi had insisted they time it so they were the last to arrive. That way the meeting could begin immediately. "Daddy always said it was the best way to make a point," she had said, and who was he to argue with her father? So he went along.

Now he could see the wisdom of her father's strategy. Every Velcro space was covered by socks and wristbands. Everyone attached so that their heads were pointed to the middle of the room. Where there was no vacant Velcro, people had looped an arm or a wristband around the support struts. All together they reminded Nathan of some underwater colony, all swaying softly in unison.

There was no place left for the two of them, so when Nathan closed the door they had to hook their wristbands around the door handle. For all the number of people there, the lounge was silent. As if they were all ready to pounce on him, Nathan thought, and he shivered. And while most were dressed in the ordinary assortment of shorts and Ts, at least five were dressed in their red uniforms.

Nathan faced that group and was suddenly shy. He didn't remember what he was supposed to do, why all these people were staring at him. Then he swallowed hard and started to talk. His voice sounded hollow and very far away.

"From the first day we reported to the selection sites in Houston or Geneva or Star City or New Delhi, we were told what we had to do to get to Mars. We had to be the best, work the hardest, pull together. We had to show that we had not only the smarts but the guts to go out and colonize a new world. Everybody in the Houston group was smart, and some of the people smarter than I didn't make it." Nathan paused to let everyone remember their own experiences. "But we're all capable and independent and not one of us will take no for an answer.

116

"And when we got to *Icarus,* we were given adult duties in ship-building and full rotation schedules. We work here just like anyone else. But we're not treated like anyone else. We aren't permitted any personal requests, our recreation preferences are ignored, even our requests to paint this lounge have been sidestepped. That isn't fair."

A murmur of assent moved through the group. But it was hesitant, grudging. Nathan realized that many of the people there hadn't thought about the things they missed from home, and the rest didn't believe they were entitled to get them.

After all, sending stuff from Earth was expensive. But sending communications, that was much easier. And food supply shuttles came in every other week. There was no reason why the group shouldn't have some say at least about what they ate.

"Yeah," Tara White agreed angrily. "You know how many newspapers are data-densed up here every day? Just check into your terminal. You got the *New York Times* and the London *Times* and *Pravda* and *Le Monde* and about ten others. Complete. And magazines on all kinds of things, news magazines, engineering, computers, even psychology. Films, music, check the menu. I did when I got here, and you know what? There were about a million things to see — if you like golden oldies. But when I asked if we could maybe add *X-Men* or *Justy* to the incoming, I got told that comics weren't permitted. Waste of money or something. Like we can get *Flying Magazine* but forget *Thrasher.*"

"And what about the fact that when we log on for games we're kicked off the system after ninety minutes of play?" Vijay asked angrily. "I know half the horticulture section plays all day. But we're supposedly tying up too much computer time. And polluting our minds."

Suddenly everyone was talking at once, telling stories about what had happened to them or their group, about the restrictions that were harsher than anything they had lived with at home. At least for some of them.

"Wait," Noemi said, but no one heard her. The noise grew, voices overlapping so that nothing at all made sense. Finally Nathan banged on the metal bulkhead hard enough to vibrate. If they couldn't hear the noise, at least they could feel the difference.

"Okay. Let Noemi have the floor," he said firmly when the din subsided.

"What we need to do now is make a very specific list of what we want and what we think is reasonable," Noemi said. "We don't

118

want to say something dumb and lose everything. The shorter and simpler the list, the better our chance of getting things. Also, if we keep it really direct, we can include a number of things in one category. Like films made for teenage audiences. That covers a lot of ground. Or space. So instead of getting angry, let's make up this list and then present it to Dr. Allen."

It didn't take long to finish the list. Cutting was harder, but they managed to keep it under ten items. "Five would be better," one of the girls in the red uniform said. "People are okay with five. Ten always feels like a lot."

With that in mind they went over the list again, but there was nothing anyone could agree to cut. They did manage to combine cookies, tortilla chips, and pizza into the single category of "high-carbohydrate snack foods."

"Yeah," one of the boys mumbled. "Call it that and we're likely to get crackers and water." So the demand was changed to "appealing and customary high-carbohydrate snack foods." And they were done.

"When should we do this?" Nathan whispered to Noemi, who seemed to have the whole attack plotted out.

"After dinner," she answered promptly.

"You, Lisette and Tara and maybe one more team leader as our representatives. When they're in the Blue lounge, where they hang out drinking coffee."

Nathan smiled. That was perfect. He found it hard to believe that Noemi had become so practical. Or maybe not. Maybe it wasn't sense the way Alice had it. But Noemi, with her wealthy and polished parents, had had opportunities he had never even dreamed of to see people high in business and government make deals over dinner.

Then Lisette caught his eye and gave him a thumbs-up. It was turning out to be the best day yet.

Chapter Eleven

Nathan never liked being on Blue deck. At first he had thought that had to do with all the supervisors having terminal time down there, but it was more than that. Blue deck didn't belong to the supervisors of the To Mars Together program either. It was home and primary work space for *Icarus*'s regular staff. Everybody in the Mars program was an intruder there, and while the regular staff had tried to make them welcome, *Icarus* was too small.

Four hundred kids and twenty adults is a lot of people right there. But *Icarus* was also supporting the crews and engineering groups working on the colony ships, and the extra modules that would supply them once they got to Mars. All the clamor and crowding of a large, important, and visible project was crammed into a station with a primary mission of pure research science.

"It's all politics," one of the astronomers had groused when Nathan and Sergei had shown up for their viewing of M-31. "We need the big, splashy projects to get funding because no one back home will vote to support pure research. Your average Joe or Ivan or Maria couldn't care less about the formation of the universe, the existence of dark matter, and whether it's a closed or open system. They want money spent on better schools and public health and subsidized housing. Something like *Icarus* isn't worth beans in their books. So we don't get money unless we can sell your basic street-level voter. And we've been reminding them of Teflon and Crazy Glue for too long."

Nathan had mumbled something like "Yeah, I guess so." It had never occurred to him that something so obviously necessary as a space station had to sell itself. The image was a little disjointed and irrational from Nathan's point of view.

The new society they built on Mars would be different. There, people would understand the need for pure research and scientists wouldn't have to prove their work was practical to get funding. Earth and the countries of Earth had messed up. This time, Nathan vowed, they were going to get it right.

Thinking about the big issues helped keep his mind off the meeting with Dr. Allen until they arrived in front of the door to the Blue deck lounge. Nathan grabbed the handle and knocked once. Hearing a voice, he swallowed hard and pushed the door open.

Inside, the place was at least three times the size of Yellow D. There were three exercycles in use, a set of zero-G climbing bars, and several groups of people playing with magnetic chess sets. A large unit dispensed coffee in squeeze bulbs, and there was a covered and anchored tray of doughnuts.

If Nathan had wondered about their list before, he was now outraged. Doughnuts. And he hadn't seen one since he'd left Earth.

It would be one thing if the goodies were for station personnel only. But in the far corner he saw Dr. Allen, one foot hooked around a support strut, watching a video game and munching on something that looked suspiciously like a honey-glazed doughnut. He launched straight over.

Mary Elizabeth Allen was not like Lawrence Thompson. Nathan had the vague impression that if Dr. Thompson found them on Blue deck, they'd be kicked out. Dr. Allen smiled and raised an eyebrow. "What's up?" she

123

asked, as if they came down to Blue lounge every day.

Nathan glanced around to find a place to hook on. He found a bit of Velcro and stepped on it lightly. The sock held. He cleared his throat.

"Uh, Dr. Allen, we, uh, that is, all the teams aboard *Icarus* had a meeting," he began. Internally he cursed himself for not coming across strong now when it counted. "You see, we recorded a music show for Gen and we were told we couldn't have it. That we couldn't ask for any entertainment or personal privileges while we were aboard *Icarus*. Even if they are harmless. If we didn't like what was here, too bad. And we don't think that's fair."

Now he was building up steam and it was a little easier. Or maybe it was because he had taken the plunge and already gotten himself into whatever trouble awaited.

To his great surprise, Dr. Allen actually smiled. "Yes, I heard about it," she said. "The problem was that you did it without authorization. We had to get retroactive permission, which, given the fact that this is a space station, wasn't too hard. Actually, the producers were rather flattered that their program had been selected by the 'space kids,' is what I think they called you."

124

Nathan was stunned. He'd been all geared up to fight, and now the whole situation was upside down. Inside out. Dr. Allen was supposed to resist their ideas, and then she would be won over by the justice of their cause. She wasn't supposed to say everything was okay.

Lisette rescued him. "We have a list of the things we'd like," the Canadian girl said agreeably. "We thought that since we got into trouble once, we'd get everything arranged beforehand."

Dr. Allen took the list, looked it over with a neutral expression. "Appealing and customary high-carbohydrate snack foods?" she asked. "You don't like the doughnuts? I'll admit they're not as fresh as you're used to, but let's give *Icarus* a break."

"We don't have any doughnuts in our lounge," Tara said innocently.

"Well, if they would be acceptable, we could get a small tray down tonight. And we'll just put it on the work order sheets, so you'll have a regular tray in Yellow D. Standard assortment agreeable?' " Dr. Allen asked, very businesslike.

"Standard assortment would be great," Nathan said.

"The rest of this isn't hard," she said, folding the list and putting it in the elastic waistband of her shorts. "Give me a day or two. I don't want to disturb the regular comm schedule."

"That's all?" Nathan asked. "I mean, with Dr. Thompson it was a federal case. Does he just hate us or something?"

Dr. Allen threw back her head and laughed. She had a very pretty laugh, Nathan thought, sort of light and bubbly. It reminded him of his mom.

"Dr. Thompson doesn't trust you," she said when she caught her breath again. "During project staff meetings he keeps telling us about how gifted kids are natural troublemakers and we'd better be careful or you might pull something really insane. It's probably because Larry used to be the worst prankster on record in the space program. But he's really proud of your work."

Lisette smiled broadly and thanked Dr. Allen for her help. But it was Nathan who pushed himself over toward the doughnuts and took two jelly-filled and one chocolate-covered. No one said anything. None of the adults even seemed to notice.

The group didn't speak until they left Blue deck. Nathan was in a daze. It had been too easy, he figured. It must have been that simple all along, only they had never thought to question the supervisor's authority. Or even to consider that there might be some differences in interpretation among the different adult project members.

A whole contingent of young astronauts was waiting in Yellow D when they returned. Nathan, Lisette, Tara and the rest kept their faces serious as they confronted their teammates. Then Nathan brought out the doughnut he hadn't eaten and threw it at Karl as if it were a Frisbee. "The rest of the tray arrives tonight," he said, and was immediately engulfed in pandemonium.

When they had finally managed to get the whole story told coherently, Lanie keyed the terminal, and the contraband transmission appeared on every monitor in the room. "Can you believe it? Everything we asked for, just like that," a British boy snapped his fingers.

"We didn't ask for anything unreasonable," Tara pointed out. "The problem was bad communication, not what we wanted."

Just then one of the regular *Icarus* staffers arrived with a clear plastic tray of doughnuts. She, or rather the snacks, were cheered loudly. The staffer winked at them broadly and then glanced at the monitors. "Hey," she said, "okay if I access this when I'm off duty?"

"Anytime," Lanie assured her, and the

woman left.

The only one who was not celebrating was Karl. He was anchored in a corner and still held the jelly doughnut, untasted, and stared at it. He was not angry, just confused. The whole structure of his life had just come down, and he was perfectly lost and alone.

For the first time in his life he had seen that playing by the rules did not mean winning. Questioning the rules had been the key. It was ugly, not harmonious, and he didn't know how the others knew when to act or even how.

Loud music and food surrounded him. It was a party, as near to one as anything could be when they all saw one another every day and no one had any good clothes and there was no chance of strangers crashing. There were no strangers aboard *Icarus*.

Karl left. He was confused and he had to think carefully. The observation port was the best place for that. This week it faced away from Earth, back out into the brilliant stars. Millions of them, hard and brittle like diamonds, stood like guardians in the dark. He knew they were all moving at fantastic speeds, whirling though the Milky Way and careening through space. But from the observation deck of *Icarus* they appeared frozen and unchanging, as they had been for centuries. His father had seen these same stars, and his grandfather, and everyone who had ever looked up at the sky.

He realized that he could choose to return to Earth. No one kept him on *Icarus*. He still could turn around and go home. He could go back to where everything made sense and he didn't have to choose between the defiance of his friends and the respect he had been brought up with. He didn't have to go to Mars.

That thought filled him with awe, with freedom. Suddenly he saw the whole mission as a crazy gamble, a useless gesture. Those stars had been there forever. On Mars his special abilities wouldn't get him the rewards he could have so easily on Earth. A good education, the title Doktor Professor, and being quoted in the national magazines. Pretty girls who would respect his talent rather than compete with him and consider him ordinary.

And there would be hardly any music on Mars. He didn't care about Gen's music, but there would be no symphony orchestras playing Beethoven, no ancient pipe organs for Bach, no great operas filling a stage with intense music and glittering costumes and even elephants.

Outside, the stars whirled through the universe, unconscious of Karl, uncaring of his existence. At the very edge of the display he saw something that twinkled red, and his mouth literally watered. Mars. There weren't any red stars in that area, that close. Ambition and sadness combined in him, and he thought he understood the heroes of the old sagas.

And then, behind him, there was music. It was as sad as he was, and as mournful. Notes tripped like water over rock in the sunlight and then faded, died.

He thought the music was just in his imagination, but he was sure he didn't know the piece and it had never been written for piano. It was more sweetly sad than any piece he knew. Slowly he turned around.

Gen drifted, one sock hooked to an anchoring strip, staring out the window and playing his rechargeable electronic guitar, Karl had never seen before. At first Karl was furious. Gen was the last person he wanted to see, ever, in the whole universe. But Gen didn't seem to notice him at all. The long-haired rocker was subdued for once, caught between the music he was playing and the vista beyond. And the music itself, merged with the grandeur of the stars and the limitations of their own lives, was too bittersweet to stop until the last echoing note had fallen.

Only when the last trace of song died away and Gen finally saw him did Karl speak. "What are you doing here?" he asked harshly.

Gen shrugged. "Same thing you are, I guess. The party and stuff, well, I just didn't feel like being around people. Like somehow I was this test case and we won something."

Karl understood. "What was that you were playing?"

"Austurius's *Alhambra,*" Gen said. "I don't play it very well. It's really hard."

"Yeah," Karl agreed. He knew about learning a hard piece, and he knew that Gen had played it, if not perfectly, at least with depth. "You have real talent."

There was a moment of silence. Karl felt as if he had just given something away and didn't know if Gen understood the value of the gift. But then Gen lowered his eyes. "Thank you," he said very softly. "Maybe sometime we should jam. Try some stuff out."

"Sometime," Karl agreed carefully. He had too much history with Gen to mend fences easily.

"You free tomorrow?" Gen asked, teasing, breaking the heavy meaning underlying their words.

"Come on," Karl said in almost his old manner. "We're on the plating crew out at the

131

Pinta tomorrow. You of all people shouldn't forget that."

"You mean you didn't check out the crew changes?" Gen asked innocently. "We're off. Got switched with Lisette's group. But we're rescheduled for the odd-day rotation now."

"I'll bet it was Sergei," Karl mumbled. "He's always chasing Lisette."

"Okay, then, it's set. Same time, same place."

Karl smiled. "It's a date . . . man."

· Chapter Twelve

Just because the schedule had been changed and they weren't outside didn't mean they weren't working. It felt like all he ever did was work. For an instant Nathan remembered warm summer evenings, the scent of hot concrete and melting ice pops, stars overhead and nothing to do. Just hanging out with friends, grousing because there wasn't anywhere to go and they couldn't get anywhere because they were all too young to drive. Sitting out at the playground while someone cranked up a boom box, talking, dreaming, when time seemed so slow.

Now time was anything but slow, and every minute of it was full, and mostly with work. At least this time it was his turn on the robot arm, along with Lanie and Sergei. Karl had had three turns in a row and then claimed experience made him the natural candidate for the job. Alice had laughed in his face and that had ended it. So Karl was with Alice on communications out to the project crews, and Gen and Noemi were both doing their usual modeling and simulation runs. They were the lucky ones, Nathan figured. They acted as though running the reliability data on the ships were better than playing the video games.

Actually, using any of the robotic attachments was sort of like a video game too. He sat in front of a large high-resolution graphics monitor that indicated the next pieces that needed to be moved, and he used a mouse to make the arm in the picture pick them up and position them in the target spot. All he did was watch the schematics on the screen go from red to green when he got it right.

The robot drones that hauled the large plates from the storage pile into position responded to Nathan's commands on microwave remote. There were four drones in all, but two were in the shop being overhauled. Each robot had its own command code repeating the microwave communications every second so that the drone responded only to their own operators. Nathan had thought it was really neat when he had first seen the system, and to be honest, it was still fun. Even if it was work.

No, if he hadn't been awake all night (or what passed for night aboard a space station) he would have felt fine. Just now he'd rather be zipped into his hammock instead of awake and concentrating.

The red went brighter, then turned dark blue as he directed the arm to pull out a sheet of plating. Blue. That was bad. It took him a moment and he blinked a few times before he realized what was wrong. Wrong piece. Wrong code number. Slowly he indicated to the arm to replace the piece and begin again.

He had to keep his mind from wandering, thinking about the night before. He forced himself to pay better attention this time, and maneuvered the arm to pick up the correct item. Then he double-checked the destination, on the hull of the *Nina*. The crew down there wasn't ready yet. That gave him a little time.

Carefully he instructed the arm to bring the oversize sheet of plating around very slowly. There was no weight in zero-G, but there was mass. And if he got a spin going on something with mass as great as that slab of metal, the sheer inertia would make it dangerous to slow down again. Once something got going without any friction from the atmosphere or gravity to slow it down, it was almost impossible to stop. And something with as much mass as that plate could do a whole lot of damage. Even kill someone.

But he couldn't keep his mind from wandering back to the night before. Specifically to after the party had ended and Yellow D had been half dark. He had thought he was alone, just thinking about how their whole little rebellion had gone so well. He'd been drifting, not anchored, and the light touch of a hand on his had startled him. He had come to with such a jerk that his own motion put him into spin.

The hand stopped that, brought him around, but didn't attach his wristband to an anchoring strip the way someone might if they wanted to talk to him.

Once he could see clearly who it was, Nathan had nearly held his breath. Lisette peeled her sock from the Velcro strip that had been holding her and, holding on to him, drifted with him.

"You know," she said softly in the semidarkness, "I think we did quite a job today."

Nathan remembered only murmuring in reply. He had been too dazed and it was too much like a dream. Reality didn't happen like this. Reality had gravity. "What about Sergei?" he had finally asked.

Lisette had closed her eyes then. "I make my own decisions," she said softly. "I don't like people who think they can own me."

They had turned on some music then, one of Nathan's favorite Sisters of Mercy CDs, the one he happened to have with him. He'd never thought of the music as romantic before. It was dark and hypnotic, Goth rock at its best, but with Lisette around, that changed. It became the right music for them, the way being weightless had become right and then natural. Then he kissed her.

Now he had a job to do, and letting his mind drift off the topic wasn't real smart. He'd already gotten into trouble once. Twice would tag him, and then someone might throw a performance rating at him. At best. At worst, well, he didn't want to think about worst.

But he was not only distracted by thoughts of the night before, he was also just plain tired. It wasn't memory that was making his eyelids droop and his head nod forward. Nathan decided that all he wanted was a nap. Just a couple of hours would be nice, only there weren't a couple of hours to spare in the workday the way it was planned. Four hours on building crew, and then he was in the gardens assisting on the feed lines. And after that was the planning session for their embarkation.

His eyes started to get heavy again and his lids slowly closed. He would have sworn it had been only a moment. No more than a blink, really. An electronic shriek brought him back to full awareness.

The robot arm was spinning slowly, way off vector, and the monitor was bleeping furiously at him. He grabbed the mouse and began trying to slow the spin down, ordering the machine to move opposite its current rotation.

But he got nowhere. Nathan felt suspended for a moment, as if this were all a dream. The robot *had* to respond. He moved the mouse again, more slowly this time.

There was no such thing as computer error. Lanie had repeated that enough times that the words made him sick. There was only operator error; only humans made mistakes. The machines didn't do anything unless a person told them to.

He tried the reset and nothing happened for a third time, so he went to "test-check." Not until the test went red did Nathan look up from his station and realize that the entire sector was in general panic. Nothing was working right, and people were frantically trying computer checks and program recalls. Every person there wore some expression of horror, and Nathan realized that he looked the same. He was frantic.

The robot was spinning out of control with a

138

huge sheet of plating in its claw. The inertia of the mass kept it going, propelling it out farther and farther into space. Another one of those electrical problems. It had to be. But this one seemed far worse, or maybe it was just because he was seeing it from the control room instead of from the outside that it seemed so pervasive.

Machines were bleeping in so many tones that it sounded like a war zone. Whatever could be done on manual already was being done. Individuals were at the ports, on the doors. Someone in an *Icarus* uniform went over and tapped Nathan on the shoulder.

"Get down to Yellow air lock," the woman said. "I think your group is concentrated there. You're the team leader, right?"

Nathan nodded, not certain what she wanted and what he had to do.

"Organize them, then," the *Icarus* official said, and wiped the hair back from her worried forehead. "There's going to be crews getting to any air lock they can by whatever means possible. Some of them could be hurt and all of them will be low on oxygen. You kids have got to cover Yellow and Red locks. We don't have enough personnel to go around if we take everything on Blue, Green, and Purple. There's too many people out there and not enough in here to help them."

Nathan nodded and was off. He didn't notice if Lanie and Sergei were following him or if they'd already gone.

He was at the Yellow air lock in four minutes. Everyone except Gen and Noemi were waiting. Their duties had been a little farther away, and with the passages so crowded it was hard for anyone to get through. Nathan took a quick glance at his teammates and at the other stragglers from different teams who had made it to the assembly point. He thought he saw Suki Long in the group but he didn't care, and he didn't have time to make sure.

"Vijay," he said, spotting another team leader in the group, "take your people up to Red air lock. And anyone else who was in the New Delhi selection group, go with them. That gives you enough?"

About twelve people in all split off. Vijay gave a thumbs-up, and that group left. "Okay," Nathan said, thinking aloud. "My team here on the air lock. We're going to have to operate this thing on manual and get people through. Then we need a team to help them out of their suits and make sure they're okay."

"We'll take care of that," Tara said firmly, since her team leader was already at her side.

"And one more group to help the injured, if

140

there are any injured," Nathan continued.

"And one more to do all the safety checks and stow the suits. Two more teams. Anyone not on one of those jobs get to Red, because I don't think they have enough help to do everything."

"And who put you in charge?" a sneering voice came from behind him.

It was Suki. Nathan was too concerned about the emergency to be bothered by her pettiness. People were in danger out there. People could die. And Lisette was out there, he realized suddenly. It was his group that had been changed with Lisette's, or else he would have been cut off, maybe hurt and unable to get back. No, he didn't have time for Suki's nonsense now.

"If you don't like it, you can go report up to Red," Nathan snapped. "Vijay'll be glad for more help." Then he turned to finalizing order at the air lock.

The lock was in fact two segments. The first was the inner door. That wouldn't open until there was enough air and pressure in the middle chamber. The middle area was what a person entered from the outer skin of *Icarus*. Every time the outer door opened, all the air in the middle chamber was immediately sucked into space. During this time the inner door had to remain sealed so that all the air in this segment of the station didn't follow.

Then both doors were sealed and new air was pumped into the middle chamber. When the pressure matched that of the rest of the space station, the inner door could be opened. That was the only way to get in and out in hard vacuum. Now, with the electronics uncertain, they had to go through the whole procedure by hand. That meant using the hand seals on the doors.

"We need someone inside," Alice said quickly. "In case whoever is out there can't open and close the seals alone."

Nathan's eyes flickered over the group. "Right. Alice, suit up. You can't work the middle chamber without a suit."

"No," Karl protested. "I should do it. I'm the strongest, and that's the hardest seal to move."

Karl was right. The locking mechanism on the outer door was large and heavy. It had never been made for human muscles to move at all, except in an emergency that everyone had dearly hoped would never happen. And Karl was the strongest, there was no denying that.

"Okay," Nathan said thoughtfully. "Karl, suit up. And then see if you can get the lock to move. If you need some help, ask. Sergei can be ready to back you up."

"Two is better anyway," Alice said firmly.

142

"It's always better to have some backup."

Nathan nodded firmly and Sergei joined Karl getting into pressure suits. Once they were changed and ready inside the chamber, Nathan and Alice took the inside lock. Gen and Lanie were in charge of the pressurized air feed, and Noemi was running the pressure read to make sure they didn't pop the door before there was enough air pressure. With everything in manual, there wasn't much space to move in and a lot to do.

The strangest part, Sergei thought afterward, was the creepy way the knocking and scratching sounded. Nothing human could have made those noises. Pressure gloves against the hull, tugging on the locking wheel, sounded like giant insects trying to invade *Icarus*.

Only they were people. Crew members and other young astronauts, all friends. And all in danger.

Sergei was glad Karl was strong. Not that Sergei was any slouch, but both of them were needed to loosen the seal around the outer door.

The first time they opened the door Sergei wasn't prepared for the power of the rush of air as it raced into the vacuum. He only hoped that whoever was on the other side hadn't been right in front of the door, or else they would have been blown halfway to Mars by the force of the rushing air. As it was, he was glad that Karl had warned him to flatten himself against the hull next to the door so they wouldn't be dragged out into the void.

Three people were waiting. Karl and Sergei helped them in. Sergei didn't notice who they were. He was only concerned that none of them seemed stable or moved steadily. If they weren't hurt, they had at least been badly shaken. Even that was dangerous in hard vacuum, where the littlest mistake meant death.

There was enough room in the chamber for three people. Karl climbed out and helped two of those waiting down to Sergei. Then he knocked on the hull and made motions that they should close the door. Sergei understood. Karl would wait with the last person. That was probably safest. The crew coming in from the emergency needed help and support.

With Karl helping turn on the outside, they got the air lock sealed quickly. Waiting in darkness seemed to last far too long. And then there was light as the inner door opened. Sergei hadn't realized when the middle chamber had reached full pressure.

Hands reached in and dragged them out. Sergei protested. Karl was still outside with the third victim. Only when they got his faceplate up and recognized him did the other team let him go.

Alone in the lock while the door shut out the light, Sergei suddenly felt afraid. He had to go alone this time to unseal the hull door. He almost didn't remember in time to get flat against the hull while the door popped and the air rushed outside. Karl helped the third person into the lock and then grabbed the wheel. Sergei was on the other side. They got the door locked, although it felt like they were moving in slow motion. The suit was bulky and Sergei could hardly feel anything in his hands. And he couldn't bend at the shoulders or elbows at all.

They got the lock closed again, and Sergei breathed hard in his helmet. He was soaked with sweat and tired. His arms and hands were chafed, his back was sore, and there was a knot at the base of his neck that wouldn't go away.

When the other team got the third victim out and were peeling off the suit, his own team helped him and Karl out of their suits. The relief was amazing. And they stank as if they had been working in the mines for weeks. Not from simple exertion, Sergei realized. The stink was fear.

145

Not until he was out of the space suit and well on the inner side of the air lock did Sergei realize just how terrified he had been. When the terror washed through him, he thought that it all had moved so slowly, it had seemed like hours. Then an announcement came over the speakers and made him jump.

"Congratulations, *Icarus*. We have not yet finished checking everyone in, but we made it through the entire air-lock drill in seven minutes. Good work."

146

Chapter Thirteen

As soon as they had finished pressurizing the compartment for the last time, Lanie went immediately to the nearest terminal to monitor check-in procedures. Even during the worst of the episodes the power-outs lasted only a few seconds. It was the havoc they caused in the unshielded machinery that created the problems.

Even though she wasn't assigned to check-in, she felt a proprietary claim. Anything to do with the computer was naturally hers, and that included all emergency procedures. She watched with pleasure as names lit up, one after another, as people fed their log-in codes into the system. For a while the board was lighting up like the Christmas display down in the mall.

And then it stopped. Everybody must be in, Lanie thought. She looked at the time check. All that activity in seven minutes. It seemed as if it had been hours, had been her whole life. She looked at the display again, scrolling down through the list of names with the log-ons recorded, and it made her feel good. Whoever thought that the bad kid from the projects would end up saving people's lives on a space station.

She scrolled and scanned unconsciously, but something just didn't seem right all of a sudden, and it sent off an alarm bell in her brain.

She went back and looked more closely, paying attention this time. And then she saw it. Lawrence Thompson had not checked in. There was no code next to his name.

Lanie stared at that for what seemed to be an eternity. Maybe it lasted less than a second. Dr. Thompson hadn't checked in? Had broken the rules? That was a new one. It took a little more for the other possibility to sink into her consciousness, and when it did she didn't hesitate. She launched out from the board and went through the corridor yelling for Nathan.

Nathan was congratulating the team on their excellent efforts when he heard his name. Lanie was soaring down the corridor yelling for him like a banshee. He froze and watched her stabilize, stick a foot out to the Velcro strip and anchor down before she told them what was going on.

"I was monitoring the check-in procedure,"

Lanie said hurriedly. "And everyone is in and the hatch is closed, and then I noticed that Dr. Thompson isn't in. He hasn't logged back."

"Maybe he just didn't get around to it yet," Noemi offered helpfully.

"Mr. Rulebook? Not likely," Lanie countered. "If he's not checked in, it's because he isn't in, and that means that something's wrong."

"Don't you think that someone else would have noticed? Someone in authority?" Karl asked.

Lanie shrugged. "Maybe. But we can't always depend on someone else catching things. If he hasn't gotten back yet, that means he can't. Either he can't get to the transport or he's hurt."

Nathan took charge. "Okay," he said firmly. "Before we suit up, we'd better check where he was working. I think Lisette said he was in their area, on the aft of the *Pinta*. I'll double-check that while the rest of you begin to suit up. And make sure those air tanks are full. We just got a lot of people out of very low tanks, and there hasn't been time to fill them all. So triple-check the ones you take."

"And we'd better take an extra in case Dr. Thompson's supply is low," Alice added.

Nathan didn't say anything. He was already gone, using powerful kicks against the walls to propel himself faster. He hoped Lisette was in

Yellow D. He figured that was where all the kids who'd been out during the emergency would go to relax and get over their experience. He understood how they felt. He only hoped someone would remember working with the missing supervisor.

Yellow D was packed when he arrived. He'd been right, everyone had gone down there to be together. After dealing with serious dangers, no one wanted to be alone. He barely got in the door when Lisette came up to him.

He didn't let her get a word out before he began. "Dr. Thompson hasn't checked in. Do you know where he was working?"

"With us," she said quickly. "On the aft section of the *Pinta,* outer hull."

Nathan took in the information and left before anyone could say anything else. There wasn't time. Every second counted. Every breath depleted the oxygen supply even further.

Most of the team was already in their suits by the time he arrived. He was able to help Noemi on with her gloves. Then he began to climb into his own suit. He remembered there was no one to help him with his helmet and gloves. No one already wearing a suit could do it very easily. He'd manage somehow.

When his helmet was fastened and the face-plate lifted, he saw Lisette. She must have followed him. She didn't say anything, just held the heavy gloves for him to stick his hands into. Then she fastened the wrist tabs to seal the unit against hard vacuum. He was ready.

"I'll take care of the air lock," Lisette said.

The speaker in the helmet was working fine. He could hear her over the electronic channels as if there had never been an interruption at all. Of course, this suit had been on *Icarus* and perhaps it hadn't been affected.

When he, Noemi, and Alice made it on the last shift through the air lock, they found the rest of the team waiting on the other side with a sled all ready to go. Karl was already locked into the steering position.

"We thought it would be easier to use the sled," Gen said cheerfully. "And there was one just around on Red lock, so we just borrowed it."

"You don't mind, Karl?" Alice asked as they locked their boots onto the sled's bed.

"Not when it means saving someone's life," Karl protested strongly. "You all locked in?"

One by one they double-checked the locks and safety lines before they confirmed. Then Karl punched in the ignition and the sled took off.

Usually Nathan loved riding the sleds. Comfortably weightless and silent in the hard vacuum, it was like effortless flying through the stars. This time, though, he wished the thing would go faster. The *Pinta* was up ahead, and it seemed to be on the other end of the solar system. And then, suddenly, they were on top of it, as Karl slowed the sled for a search pattern.

He circled the aft section of the hull twice very carefully, but there was no sign of Dr. Thompson. The *Pinta* had only half its skin on at this point. The rest of it was a gaping black hole.

"Inside," Alice said.

Karl swung the sled around. Alice was right, that was the first place to look. But a knot formed in Nathan's stomach as they entered the unfinished side of the colony ship. There was something derelict about it, something that made him think of the evil things that could be there, all the slasher movies he had laughed at with Eddie and the gang back at home. Only this wasn't a movie and it sure wasn't home.

Inside the ship the sled's powerful search beam wasn't lost in the infinities of space. Here it illuminated the pristine, nearly finished supply bay. Mostly to Nathan's unpracticed eye it looked pretty well done, ready to go.

"Let's take it slow," he found himself saying calmly. "We don't want to miss him because we're impatient." The words had come out of his mouth, but Nathan wasn't sure why he'd said them. It wasn't like him at all. It sounded more like his chemistry teacher. Well, that wasn't important. What was important was the search.

Very methodically Karl used the beams to light segments of the inner walls. Section after section of the bay fell under their scrutiny.

Gen spotted it first, a shadow that was a little irregular, that was not the straight and geometric patterns of the ship. They closed in carefully, and as they approached, the shadow resolved into the figure of a space suit. A very large space suit.

Dr. Thompson had tied his safety line to a rung on the wall. Karl slowed the sled so that it was almost drifting. "I'm going to come in very close," he said. "Sergei, cut the safety line and catch the end of it. The rest of you pull him in. We can tie the line to the frame if we have to."

There was no chatter about the plan. Like a dream in perfect silence, Karl nudged the sled so it was drifting just under the helpless astronaut's body. "What do I cut with?" Sergei asked, panicked.

Something flashed like liquid silver. A switchblade appeared in Lanie's gloved hand. She tried to reach to cut the safety line, but she was too short. She handed the knife to Sergei. His three extra inches made all the difference. He was able to hold the line and cut at the same time. And then he dragged the cut line down with Dr. Thompson on the other end.

Alice tied the line in a strong knot. They tried to look at he supervisor, but they couldn't see behind the reflective sunshield. And he drifted as if he were unconscious. "He has only twenty minutes of air left," Alice announced.

But Karl was already taking the sled out of the *Pinta* and steering back to the Yellow air lock on *Icarus*.

As Alice and Gen took Dr. Thompson through the air lock, Nathan and Karl secured the sled. By the time they had the sled ready, it was the next group's turn to enter the station, and Nathan went with Noemi and Sergei.

He arrived to see Alice tugging frantically on Dr. Thompson's space suit. "It won't come off," she moaned, and pulled again on the wrist tabs. "Where's that knife?"

But Lanie was still outside with Karl. Nathan was wondering where the emergency medical team was. There should be someone here already, in case Dr. Thompson was in worse shape than they could handle.

But Noemi was smiling. She already had her helmet and gloves off. She reached down under the T-shirt she was wearing inside the space suit and pulled out a fortune in diamonds. That stupid necklace. She wore it even when they were wearing pressure suits on a rescue mission.

Noemi handed the necklace to Alice. "Use these," the Venezuelan girl said.

As Nathan watched, Alice used the faceted diamonds to shred the heavy fabric of the pressure suit. Made to withstand most things, the suit could not hold out against the hardest substance in the universe. It fell in ribbons around the supervisor, chips and wires exposed as fresh air circulated around the ashen skin. Unable to get the helmet off, Alice simply cut off the section below the coupling joint and took off the whole assembly.

Dr. Thompson was still breathing. In fact, his coloring was rapidly becoming more normal and his eyes fluttered. He was coming around when the emergency team arrived from medical.

The whole thing was definitely very weird, Nathan thought. Dr. Thompson was actually happy to see them, and Nathan was glad to see the supervisor in such good health.

They had saved their supervisor's life. The medical team told them later that while the air supply was not bad, Dr. Thompson had hit the apparatus against the wall when he was jerked around during the emergency and a valve had bent. Now Dr. Thompson looked like he was ready to take on the Martian Olympic team. Or lead it.

"Sunspots," he was saying. "I had this funny feeling about them. They are correlated to erratic electronics, but no one knows why. It's not like a solar flare or an electromagnetic pulse. They come in eleven-year cycles."

"And that's what caused all the electrical interference with our radios and equipment and everything?" Noemi asked.

"Exactly," Dr. Thompson said. "But we're at the end of a cycle now and shouldn't have any problems before launch date. And, speaking of which, I was checking your work logs yesterday and . . ."

Nathan and the rest of the team groaned.

". . . just wanted to say that you're doing a good job. Of course, your response time on lock maneuvers was down in this little rescue mission, and using a switchblade to cut the cable was totally against E.V.A. space procedure. But I wouldn't be here right now without your help, so I guess I'll let it all slide—this time." He paused, looking at his team of young astronauts. "Just do me one favor. Stay out of trouble until our launch date, okay?"

"Trouble, Dr. Thompson? Us?" Lanie asked sweetly.

SUIT UP WITH NATHAN AND HIS TEAM OF YOUNG ASTRONAUTS AS THEY BLAST THEIR WAY THROUGH A DANGEROUS ASTEROID BELT ON THEIR WAY TO MARS IN THE NEXT EXCITING SPACE ADVENTURE:
THE YOUNG ASTRONAUTS #4: DESTINATION: MARS!

Follow the odyssey . . .

Blast off with Nathan, Sergei, Lanie, Noemi, Alice, Gen and Karl on their future adventures in outerspace—a new one every other month!

January, 1991:
THE YOUNG ASTRONAUTS #4:
DESTINATION MARS

March, 1991:
THE YOUNG ASTRONAUTS #5:
SPACE PIONEERS

May, 1991:
THE YOUNG ASTRONAUTS #6:
CITIZENS OF MARS

Look for them at your local bookstore.
Be sure to collect the whole series including:
THE YOUNG ASTRONAUTS
THE YOUNG ASTRONAUTS #2:
READY FOR BLASTOFF!

For more information about The Young Astronaut
Council, or to start a Young Astronaut Chapter in
your school, write to:

THE YOUNG ASTRONAUT COUNCIL
1211 Connecticut Avenue, N.W.
Suite 800
Washington, D.C. 20036